Y0-ARH-693

SOUTHERN YANKEES

SOUTHERN YANKEES

by

HELEN R. SPEICHER
and
KATHRYN K. BORLAND

illustrated by

INGRID FETZ

Printed in the United States of America
Library of Congress Catalog Number: 60-14549

For two patient husbands
and six impatient children
from two provoking wives.

Contents

CHAPTER		PAGE
1	The Cartwrights of Missouri	9
2	The Cartwrights of Virginia	15
3	Twinoaks	21
4	War Clouds	33
5	April Twelfth	47
6	The Map	59
7	The Red, White and Gray	69
8	Of Needling and Needles	81
9	The Underground Railway	93
10	Quaker Hospitality	103
11	Of Rain and Runaways	117
12	Potions and Poultices	127
13	Hide and Seek	135
14	Tom Scores His Point	145
15	Fire!	153
16	It's William's Move	161
17	Swing Low, Sweet Chariot	169
18	Two Southern Yankees	185

1

XXXXXX

The Cartwrights of Missouri

"AND THINGS just never were the same after the war," Aunt Hattie Lou's voice droned on.

John muttered something to the effect that he would never be the same either, and Ann gave him a warning nudge, although she couldn't help feeling that he was probably right. For one thing, she knew her feet were at least two sizes larger from seeing every relic in Washington left from the War Between the States. Every moth-eaten Confederate soldier's suit, every Southern belle's diary, every Confederate general's sword had been seen once, and some of them twice.

Spending spring vacation in Washington with

Aunt Hattie Lou had seemed such a wonderful idea when she wrote to their mother about it, but they should have paid more attention to that ominous little phrase: "They should know more of their background as Cartwrights of Virginia."

From seven o'clock in the morning, when Aunt Hattie Lou came pattering in on her determined little feet to start them on their day's round of sight-seeing, until ten o'clock at night when they fell exhausted into their beds, Aunt Hattie Lou had kept up a relentless commentary on the War Between the States and the Cartwrights in Virginia.

"If I didn't know better, I'd think the South had won," John said one night.

"If they didn't, it's certain Aunt Hattie Lou thinks they ought to have," Ann agreed. "We're probably the only people who ever came to Washington and didn't see the Lincoln Memorial."

But now they were in the taxi on their way to the station, and the War Between the States would soon be ended for the second and, they hoped, final time.

The warm April sun was making Ann drowsy, but she could hear Aunt Hattie Lou's voice, as though from a great distance, saying, "And when our officers came back, that wicked girl told them she had put the map up the chimney. If she hadn't been Jefferson Cartwright's niece and only twelve years old—just your age—it's hard to say what might have happened to her.

" 'It's up the chimney,' she said, bold as brass. Of course it was better to burn it than to turn it over to the Yankees, which she might have tried to do. At least, after she disappeared, nobody really knew but what . . ."

This was the first story that had interested Ann and John to any marked degree, but the taxi was drawing up in front of the station and, as Aunt Hattie Lou did not believe in tipping taxicab drivers and liked to explain why, the twins, who had suffered through several embarrassing scenes during the week, quickly withdrew to wait for her on the station steps.

Ann looked approvingly at her reflection in one of the glass doors. Ordinarily clothes were of little concern to her, but she did feel distinguished in her gray suit and jaunty red hat.

John said, "Tomorrow we'll be the Cartwrights of Missouri. No more cannons, no more fried chicken or candied yams." John hated fried

chicken, and ate it only when politeness or his mother made it necessary.

"I can wear jeans and ride Major," Ann said. "No more Uncle Jeff Cartwright and Aunt Caroline Cartwright and the little Cartwrights."

Aunt Hattie could be heard telling the taxi driver that she wished him a good day. "It ain't at all likely with the start I got, ma'am," the driver replied, driving off with more speed than usual.

"Of course you really can't expect taxi drivers to be as courteous as the old coachmen used to be," Aunt Hattie Lou remarked as she climbed briskly up the steps. "How many times I recall hearing my mother tell how her Uncle Jeff's coachman, old Lafe, used to sweep off his tall beaver hat and stand, even in the pouring rain, waiting for them to . . ."

But the twins had put on polite expressions and closed their ears to old Lafe. By the time Aunt Hattie Lou had finished the story about his saving Susan Cartwright from a runaway horse, it was time for Ann and John to tell Aunt Hattie truthfully that they would never forget this week spent with her, and they were soon going through the gates to the train.

"How about ten minutes of quiet?" asked John when they had found their seats on the north side of the train.

"All right, but I'll know if you're even thinking about the War," Ann said.

"Don't worry; I won't be," her brother assured her.

Ann looked at him with pleasure. Most people don't admit to anything so unbelievable as liking a brother, but Ann and John had a great deal in common. They liked the same people and thought the same things were funny. She even thought him rather nice-looking—maybe because they were twins.

The sun, which had made her drowsy in the taxicab, was having the same effect in the train, and this time Aunt Hattie Lou's voice was not there to prod her awake.

2

xxxxxx

The Cartwrights of Virginia

ANN SHIVERED slightly. This train had not seemed drafty when they first found their seats. Unwillingly her brown eyes opened from the brief nap, and in utter horror caught a glimpse of lace ruffles stirring across her legs. Lace ruffles? Furtively Ann investigated. They were firmly sewn on—on pantalettes. And she, Ann Cartwright, was wearing them.

Unbelievingly, Ann moved first one leg and then the other. Both were surrounded by a froth of ruffles. A pair of gray cloth boots buttoned primly up the side over her ankles. Her very full skirt was still of gray flannel, but it covered several stiff petticoats. Her gray coat was three-quarter length, with wide-draped sleeves trimmed in maroon braid. Reaching up, Ann felt a bonnet on her head, tied under her chin with matching maroon ribbons of silk.

"This is a silly dream, and I'll wake up if I pinch myself hard," she said half aloud. However, the gray mitts on her hands made this rather difficult. "Trips to Aunt Hattie Lou will have to stop," she murmured, glancing over at John.

To Ann's astonishment, John was wearing a gray flannel suit with long trousers that narrowed down around his ankles, a black vest, a white shirt ruffled down the front, and a short red tie. Worst of all were the knee-length black cloak and small, stiff black hat. This was too absurd!

Suddenly John was awake. "Jeepers, I'm glad you woke me. I dreamed I was living during the War Between the States. Of course I realize it was just because we've heard about nothing else for the last two weeks, but— What's the matter? You look funny."

Smiling at John's understatement, Ann said, "Maybe we're just figments of each other's imaginations." And they continued to stare at each other.

Then, with bewildered faces, they stared around them. The luxurious parlor car they had boarded at the station had become a narrow-aisled, plush-seated conveyance that bumped annoyingly. The single-paned windows let in gusts of chilly air and framed an unfamiliar landscape. The rolling hills seemed strangely deserted. There were no billboards, no busy, car-patrolled roads, no planes in the sky.

Ann looked down at her tapestry pocketbook with its wooden handles and said, "The whole thing is just too fantastic. We must be dreaming."

"Listen," John said excitedly, "we couldn't both be dreaming the same thing. I think we must be displaced in time."

"What's that?" asked Ann, staring unhappily at her buttoned boots.

"My science teacher says some people have a theory that it may be possible to project yourself into some other time."

"Without even trying?" Ann asked incredulously.

"Aunt Hattie Lou may have pushed us," John said. "Naturally I don't really believe it, but what fun if we were."

"Well, before we gallop off in all directions let's be sure we really aren't dreaming," Ann suggested sensibly.

"All right. You pinch me and I'll pinch you," was John's cheerful idea.

"I'd even try one of your pinches to wake up," Ann agreed. But hard as he pinched, nothing was changed. "Ouch! You didn't have to draw blood," she protested.

"Well, you didn't have to kick me, either," John answered.

"If we ever get back, you can tell your science teacher he was right," Ann said, "because we certainly seem to be awake."

"In that case, let's ask the conductor where we get off," John said practically.

He half rose to get the conductor's attention, and the tall man soon stood at his side.

"Could you please tell us when we will arrive at our station?" asked John politely.

"Same time as usual, Master John," was the surprising answer. "We're a shade late because we had to stop and cut some more firewood for the engine, but we should be in Fairfield before dusk."

"Thank you," replied John. "Can you tell us the

time, please? Our wrist watches seem to have stopped."

"Your what?"

"Our wrist watches," repeated John, pulling at the cuff of his shirt. But there was nothing on his wrist, and he could see Ann shake her head slightly. Of course, they wouldn't have wrist watches.

The conductor was looking oddly at him, so he smiled and yawned and said sleepily, "Guess I'm not quite awake yet." It seemed to be a satisfactory answer.

"Better get your packages together, Miss Ann," the conductor advised. "Since it's the end of the line everybody will be wanting to get off first, and you know Mr. Cartwright doesn't like to be kept waiting." With that, he hurried down the aisle.

"How did he know us? Or that Uncle Jefferson's name was Cartwright?" demanded Ann, careful to keep her voice low.

"And where is this Fairfield?" countered John.

"How could you possibly forget that the Cartwright plantation was in Virginia!" Ann said.

The other passengers were stirring in obvious preparation to leave the train, and John and Ann watched them, fascinated. The women wore poke bonnets of material to match their cloaks, and among the men there was not a clean-shaven face.

"Let's wait until everybody's off the train and see if a modern conductor won't shake us awake," Ann suggested hopefully.

But, as the train began to clear, the conductor motioned impatiently to them, and the twins moved slowly toward the door with the feeling that the future held more uncertainty than they cared to discover.

3

XXXXXX

Twinoaks

As THE twins moved down the aisle, Ann's arm was still red from the pinching John had given it, and John's ankle ached fiercely. But they still could not escape the feeling that they were in a dream.

A tiny woman with piercing black eyes was pushing her way past others in the aisle, heedless of dropped packages and disapproving looks.

"I declare," she said breathlessly, when she was close enough to clutch each twin by the arm with a black-gloved hand, "you two surely have grown since you were here last summer, but I knew John right away because he's still the very image of his Uncle Jefferson.

"Your Aunt Caroline told me about you comin' to stay and your mother bein' sick and all, but I thought maybe you wouldn't come now, things bein' the way they are. I suppose Lafe will be here to get you, and like as not Susan and Tom. Of course Belle's gotten past the point where she goes every time the carriage comes around."

She seemed suddenly aware of the bewilderment in the eyes of her captives.

"You do remember me, don't you? Mrs. Hurley?"

"Oh, yes, ma'am," Ann heard herself saying. She didn't ordinarily say "ma'am." Evidently she was going to know how to talk, and that was a relief.

It didn't take much conversation to satisfy Mrs. Hurley. Her voice—which was soft yet somehow disagreeable, like the whine of an unseen mosquito—was droning on.

"I was visitin' my sister in North Carolina, but what with all the talk of firin' on Fort Sumter any day now, I decided not to stay any longer. Isn't it thrillin'? My goodness, if they do go ahead and do it, and it surely looks as if they will, you may be down here quite a while.

"And I suppose," she said thoughtfully, "you could be classed as Yankees, Missouri not rightly bein' able to make up its mind. Naturally your mother doesn't feel that way or she wouldn't have sent you here."

She stopped, and from the arch of her eyebrows they knew that she had asked them a question. At that moment her attention was fortunately distracted by the conductor, who asked her to point out her portmanteau.

"Looks as if we're back in the War Between the States," John whispered to Ann.

"Fort Sumter," Ann hissed back. "Which side fired on it?"

John gave her a scornful look. "Great," he said. "I told you you ought to read more history and less *Alice in Wonderland.*"

They stepped down from the train, and a tall Negro resplendent in blue broadcloth and silver buttons came toward them. Beside him, her feet hardly seeming to touch the ground, was a small pixie of a girl, about eight years old, with long curls and a freckled face.

"Cousin Ann!" she shrieked excitedly. At the same moment the toe of her buttoned black boot caught in one of the cracks of the wooden platform, and she fell flat on her face.

This accident was unfortunate, but it did eliminate the necessity of any greeting on the part of the twins. By the time the small girl had recovered from her fall, they had learned that she was Susan, and that the tall, dark-haired boy standing quietly in the background was Tom.

"Lafe," Mrs. Hurley said, "I didn't have time to let anybody know I was comin', and I'm so tired from that dreadful trip I thought I could just ride as far as Twinoaks with you now, and Bucky can pick me up later. You could ride on over and tell him I'm there."

"Surely, ma'am," Lafe replied easily.

The twins' hearts sank. Their first conversation with their supposedly beloved cousins would have to be carried on under the gimlet eye of Mrs. Hurley.

They need not have worried, for the moment they were seated in the carriage Mrs. Hurley began questioning Susan and Tom about their older sister, Belle, and her beaus. Mrs. Hurley apparently did not approve of Belle's favorite beau—William.

Ann and John were left free to concentrate on the beautiful but unfamiliar scenery. They soon noticed that the carriage was turning into a curved driveway, at the end of which stood an imposing red brick house with white pillars across the front. A beautiful lawn stretched out as far as they could see in every direction.

"Golly," Ann breathed, "it looks just like a movie."

Mrs. Hurley paused in mid-sentence and turned toward her quickly. "Speak up, child," she said. "A lady doesn't mumble her words. Now, say it again properly."

Ann thought quickly; a movie would be hard to explain. "It looks just as I thought it would," she offered.

"Well, I should think so." Mrs. Hurley sniffed. "It could hardly have changed much since last summer."

Mrs. Hurley set about instructing Lafe how to carry her numerous boxes and bundles, and Ann and John followed Susan and Tom to the house. A small, pretty, brown-haired woman in a white dress with a sweeping skirt stepped out on the porch, and Ann felt that if this smiling person were Aunt Caroline everything would surely be all right.

"Ann and John! How well you look, and how

glad we are to have you," she said, hugging each in turn. Her voice was soft, too, but her accent was beautiful, Ann thought.

"I am so anxious to hear all about your mother, but you are later than we had thought, and Uncle Lawrence is comin' for dinner, so you had better go to your rooms and wash up as quickly as possible. This evenin' we'll have all the time in the world to talk."

As she spoke she showed them into a square hall larger than their living room at home.

"Come on, Ann." Susan raced up the curving

stairway ahead of her, and Ann followed as best she could, hoping she was not to be condemned to wear ten pounds of petticoats for the rest of her life.

"You're goin' to be in my room this time," Susan pronounced. "Belle wouldn't share her bureau drawers with anybody. She's so fussy, and no fun at all any more. All the time gettin' laced and curled, and always washin'. I hope I never grow up, don't you?"

She ushered Ann into a room which made her gasp because it was so perfect. The huge four-poster bed was topped with a ruffled white organdy canopy matching the dust ruffle and the crisp curtains at the window. The carpet on the floor was covered with tiny red roses, and bigger roses blossomed on the quilt that covered the bed. A huge mahogany bureau with the drawers open stood between two windows which looked out over the driveway.

Ann was crossing the room to look out the window when there was a knock at the door, and a low, husky voice said, "It's Aunt Phoebe."

Ann's heart sank. Another aunt, and mention of another uncle yet to come. She would never master this complex household. But to her surprise Aunt Phoebe turned out to be a tall, pleasant-looking Negro woman.

"You *are* a sight for sore eyes, Miss Ann," she said, "and prettier every time you come. I brought your portmanteau up case there was anything you want, but we unpacked your trunk when it came yesterday. Mr. Lawrence is comin' for dinner, so put on somethin' pretty."

She opened the doors of a heavy mahogany wardrobe, and Ann saw a bewildering number of beruffled, besashed dresses of every color hanging inside. What would she be likely to wear? Aunt Phoebe was waiting.

Ann's heart sank as she thought longingly of blue jeans and shorts and sleeveless blouses and tailored skirts—of anything that didn't have fifty yards of ruffles and touch her shoe tops.

"Oh, wear this one, Ann." Susan solved her immediate problem by selecting a thin white dress with tiny embroidered lavender flowers and a stiff lavender sash.

Suddenly Phoebe exclaimed, "I forgot about ironin' Miss Belle's pink lawn. You'll be all right, won't you, Miss Ann?"

Miss Ann doubted it, but she smiled uncertainly at Phoebe's broad back.

"Well, hurry up, slowpoke," Susan said. "Aren't you goin' to wash before you get dressed?"

"Of course," Ann answered. "Where's the bathroom?"

"Bathroom? You don't have a special room to take a bath in at your house, and you know it. Your house isn't even as big as ours."

While Susan was talking she poured some water from a china pitcher with red roses painted on it into a matching bowl which stood on a marble-topped chest in one corner of the room.

Ann stuck her finger into the lukewarm pool of water and tried not to think of a hot shower. While she was laboriously washing one piece of herself at a time she thought she might as well try to fit some more pieces into the puzzle, but it was hard to frame questions which would give her the answers she needed and still not make Susan suspicious.

"What's Uncle Lawrence doing these days?" Ann asked as she scrubbed her neck vigorously to hide her nervousness.

"He's bein' the editor of his newspaper in town

same as he was last year and every year before that forever," Susan answered. "Mrs. Hurley says she thinks it's a queer occupation for a gentleman, but I don't know why. It's always so busy there, and even smells excitin'. I like it, especially since William is there. He's ever so nice. Belle's sweet on William, and so am I. If she doesn't marry him, I think I will."

All that information from just one question, thought Ann happily. "Why doesn't Mrs. Hurley like William?" she asked, taking advantage of Susan's talkative mood.

"Oh, her," Susan said contemptuously. "She doesn't really like anybody much, but she specially doesn't like William because his mother was from up North. But William's father is a Culpeper, and everybody thought it was all right for him to marry whom he wanted. William even went to a Yankee college and nobody cared, but lately everybody's started sayin' horrible things about William that Father won't even let us repeat in this house."

Ann finished her bath and struggled into the scratchy pantalettes Aunt Phoebe had laid out on the bed before she left. Why did everything have to be starched, she wondered. When she walked, it sounded like someone reading the evening paper.

She was gathering up courage to raise the hot stiff petticoat over her head, when the door flew open and the most beautiful girl Ann had ever seen rushed into the room and hugged her.

"Ann, Ann," she said, laughing, "you really look lovely, even if you do have your pantalettes on backwards." Her laugh was so infectious that Ann did not feel embarrassed.

This must be Belle. She was tall and had shining golden hair drawn back into ringlets at the back of her neck. She was wearing something beautiful and pink and smelled deliciously of lavender.

"Here, I'll help you into your petticoat and then you can turn them around," Belle said. She darted around the room, admiring Ann's lavender-sprigged dress, tying the sash, finding a pair of lavender kid slippers which looked infinitely more comfortable than the high-buttoned gray boots, and making Ann feel less alone than she had felt since this whole unbelievable thing had happened.

In fact, walking down the stairs in Belle's wake. Ann was surprised to find that she felt a thrill of anticipation instead of fear about what might happen next.

4

XXXXXX

War Clouds

JOHN WAS relieved to hear the soft chimes summoning them to dinner. Tom had given him a bad half hour with his questions about his school year, and he felt as if he were balancing on a tightrope.

In contrast to his gloomy mood, the girls frothed out of Susan's room, down the winding stairway, laughing gaily. John watched them, their full skirts as colorful as flower petals, and his spirits rose a little in answer to Ann's lilting smile. Blue jeans had their place, but he had to admit those soft colors and ruffles brought out the girl in a girl.

After all, there were advantages to being displaced backward in time. They would be much

more likely to know some of the answers in the schoolroom. And maybe they could invent some indispensable gadget and make a lot of money. John began to wish he'd paid more attention to the construction of the many zippers he had used.

"What's that super smell?" John asked as they neared the dining room.

"What's 'super'?" and Susan glanced at him in surprise. Then, luckily not waiting for an explanation, she answered, "Fried chicken and candied yams, of course, since Uncle Lawrence is comin' to dinner and those are his favorites, too."

Shades of Aunt Hattie Lou! thought John rebelliously. I've heard about Southern fried chicken for two weeks. I've had to eat it for two weeks, and now I suppose I'll have to live on it until the war is over!

"Don't you remember how last year you and he had a contest one day when Mother and Belle were out callin'?" Susan continued. "You wanted to see which one of you could eat the most chicken, and he won. But he said he'd never bet that with you again, 'cause you'd be able to eat him under the table this year."

John's face reddened. This Susan would take a

bit of getting used to, and he wondered if she could cause trouble for them. She could! They'd have to watch their speech in front of her. In back of her too, most likely.

"Susan, shame!" Belle reproved her gently. "Cousin John's just now come. Don't spoil his visit by pesterin' him the way you did last year."

Tom led them into the dining room where the long table, glowing with a white damask cloth and gleaming with the reflections of many candles on the silver and porcelain, was flanked by five adults. Soft lights from lamps on the mahogany sideboard gave the room a warm and inviting look.

A tall, slender young man nodded to John and Ann with a pleasant smile, then turned his attention to Belle. This must be William, the twins deduced, glad he seemed friendly.

But to their dismay, standing by the side of the tall blond man who was obviously Uncle Lawrence, was Mrs. Hurley. She'd not miss a trick, and the twins silently vowed to speak as seldom as possible.

Uncle Jefferson, immaculate in white linen and very much the picture of a Southern plantation owner, reminded them immediately of their own dark-eyed mother. Turning to them, he commented graciously, "This is a gala occasion, and since Mrs. Hurley knew your mother before she married and moved to Missouri we've urged our neighbor to join us for dinner."

She'd take about as much urging as a starving lioness offered a raw T-bone steak, thought Ann anxiously. Why couldn't it just be family tonight? That would be hard enough.

"Shall we sit down?" asked Aunt Caroline. "Ann, you come over here to my right. Susan's been beggin' all day to sit next to you, and Belle, maybe you can keep Susan from makin' a question mark of herself and entertain William at the same time. John, you and Tom can talk all you want to each other, with your Uncle Jefferson at the end to see you don't starve to death. Now, Mrs. Hurley, you will have a gentleman on either side of you."

Ann knew John was struggling to repress a giggle as they watched Mrs. Hurley tap Uncle Lawrence playfully on the sleeve with her fan.

As soon as everyone was seated, smoking hot platters of fried chicken, steaming dishes of buttery yams and hot dishes of okra and black-eyed peas, both dishes new to the twins, were served by attentive slaves wearing the same colored livery that Lafe had worn, and conversation was limited to expressions of pleasure.

John lost count after the fourth kind of pickles was passed, but was ready for the strawberry jam and quince jelly that accompanied the hot biscuits with their golden crusts.

John leaned back in his chair finally and beamed at Aunt Caroline. "If I never eat again it won't make a bit of difference," he assured her, averting his eyes from the chicken platter. John had long since discovered that women like to be complimented on the meals they serve, and he found that good manners didn't interfere with his enjoyment of a hearty meal.

"Law, child, you haven't changed a bit! You always did like to eat," Aunt Caroline said, smiling happily at him. "But what's happened to your appetite for chicken? You used to eat so much I was afraid you'd begin to cackle instead of talk."

John joined in the laughter directed at him, and to change the topic of conversation he asked half-jokingly, "Tom, how come you're not as big as the Statue of Liberty, with all these good things to eat?"

“The what?” queried Uncle Lawrence.

Frantically John’s mind raced. The Statue of Liberty wasn’t even built until 1880 something—uh, 1886, he remembered belatedly.

“Oh, I forgot, you haven’t seen it yet.” No, that wasn’t the right thing to say. He tried again, almost stammering in his effort to make conversation that wouldn’t damage them so soon in their acquaintance with these new relatives. “It’s an enormous statue 301 feet high in the New York harbor.”

He could feel Ann’s sympathy reaching out to him as she added quickly, “We haven’t seen it either, but there’s been some talk in Missouri about how big it is, and I’m with John, not being able to imagine you staying so thin with biscuits like these within easy reach. Mother hasn’t baked since she’s been ill, and my cornbread makes John reach for a second piece of something else.”

Then, turning to Belle, she changed the subject firmly. “Do you like to cook?” she asked.

“Why, no.” Belle was surprised. “I haven’t been out in the kitchen since I used to steal hot cookies, and now Aunt Sarah’s so old and cross everybody leaves her alone.”

Uncle Lawrence laughed softly. "Belle is a recent addition to our social life, and well named."

Belle blushed prettily, but regained her composure quickly. "I declare to goodness, Uncle Lawrence, you're the biggest tease in all the county."

Her father joined in the laughter, adding, "And Jester can yap all he wants to; we'll just ignore him."

Then the family began recalling the reason for their pet's name—how his worried barking had aroused the entire plantation one night soon after Mr. Cartwright had brought him home. Thinking their new watchdog had flushed an intruder, Uncle Jefferson had rushed outdoors, shotgun in hand, to find that one of Belle's escorts, returning her from a dance, had stopped the carriage halfway down the lilac-lined drive. Belle's disgusted glance sent her father quickly back to the house, and from then on the dog's name was Jester and his barking was seldom heeded.

William smiled at Belle, and they both seemed to indicate that all that had happened a long time previously.

During dessert—a delicious pecan pie too rich to eat quickly—John became aware that the three men were quieter and more serious in their speech than was apparently their custom. Aunt Caroline met the situation with an order for the candles to be trimmed and a request that Mr. Cartwright remember he had several guests to entertain who might not share his fondness for politics.

Mrs. Hurley countered with a small sniff and decreed that politics was everyone's business, especially when the South had been insulted and her states' rights questioned.

"A difference of opinion needn't cause a war," Mr. Cartwright said tolerantly. "It's true the South seems to be sort of a stepsister at the moment, but hot heads and hot words can fan a flame that could be as easily extinguished with cold logic."

"The South is poorly prepared to wage a war now," elaborated Lawrence Preston. "It would be the height of folly at the present time, when we have so few woolen mills, cotton factories and iron foundries. And can you name a cannon factory south of the Mason-Dixon line? All we have are cotton and slaves, and not a single warship. If the Yankees patrolled our harbors, we couldn't even sell our cotton abroad."

Mrs. Hurley, her face pink with emotion, said

shrilly, "The very reason I came home was for fear Fort Sumter might be fired on. My sister Georgia —the one who lives on Charleston Bay—says everyone's nerves have been on edge since January. That's when the *Star of the West*, carrying provisions to the Fort, was fired on. We'd rather see the Stars and Bars—that the Confederate Convention decided on last month at Montgomery—flying above the fort than that Union flag."

Uncle Lawrence's face was grim. "Much public sentiment joins you there. Seven states have already seceded from the Union."

"But why does it have to end in war?" Uncle Jefferson said. "We're living in a civilized country. Why must these hotheads plunge us into a turmoil the majority doesn't want?"

Mrs. Hurley answered crisply, "From the looks of the uniforms and the number of soldiers drilling everywhere, I'd say the majority not only wants war, but is ready for it."

"A blue cockade in a cap and a red sash don't necessarily make a soldier," Uncle Lawrence replied sadly. "And what I deplore most is the downright suspicion that's beginning to come between even close friends."

"A friend is someone you can trust," snapped Mrs. Hurley, glancing at William meaningly, "and I surely couldn't trust a person who didn't know which side he was on."

William's gray eyes met hers steadily, but there was the tinge of embarrassment on his cheeks.

Then, as another thought came to her, Mrs. Hurley continued, "If Ben Holmes doesn't stop talkin' about brotherly love he's goin' to lose all his friends, even if he is a Quaker. It's a cryin' shame the way he talks. He even thinks everyone should read that book, *Uncle Tom's Cabin*."

Only Uncle Lawrence had the courage to stem her flow of words. Briefly he agreed, "Yes, if Ben Holmes weren't so well liked he'd have had a bad time in town this morning."

Mrs. Hurley turned briskly to William, and before Belle could intercede she asked intently, "Now, young man, you're strong and able to fight. What do you plan to do when a Confederate Army is formed?" She was obviously enjoying the discomfort of everyone at the table, for they all liked William, whatever his convictions.

William, although his knuckles whitened, won the twins' instant approval by returning Mrs. Hurley's malicious gaze calmly and answering honestly, "It would be difficult for me to leave all this to fight a senseless war."

"Maybe you'll be surprised," needled Mrs. Hurley, "at the number of states that will use good sense and leave the Union. Just because you went to school in the North, you needn't think Southern spirit has died out. It's men like you——"

"Unfortunately," interrupted Uncle Jefferson, "there's spirit enough to make this situation quite explosive. In my opinion, Fort Sumter will be fired on. And it may be soon."

John managed a glance at Ann. Her face was paper white, so she was wondering the same thing he was. What was the date Fort Sumter had been fired on? He'd wager she was wishing she'd paid closer attention in history class.

John could almost see his history book—the page with the date of those tragic shots that preceded the devastating War Between the States. April 1861? The twelfth? Yes, that sounded right. Then what was the date this evening? It had been April eleventh when they'd left Washington!

John was suddenly startled to hear his name, as Mr. Cartwright asked him kindly, "Just what are your Mother's friends saying in Missouri, John? Although a boy your age probably doesn't care much about politics."

If you only knew how much I do care, John thought, but he answered carefully, "Well, feeling is divided."

This seemed the answer Uncle Jefferson expected, for he remarked, "I suppose many men there who own no slaves think slavery is a terrible thing. Others have moved into Missouri bringing their slaves with them, and consequently can see no wrong in slavery."

John wondered how such obviously kind and intelligent gentlemen as Jefferson Cartwright and Lawrence Preston could believe that slavery was a good thing.

But Aunt Caroline was giving the signal to leave the table. The strained, white faces of the twins had not escaped her notice, and wishing their first evening to end on a pleasant note, she announced clearly, "All this is hardly table talk for children. You men finish your conversation in the library, and tomorrow, Ann and John, we'll have a real talk about your poor mother."

To Mrs. Hurley's obvious disappointment, Mrs.

Cartwright ordered Lafe to bring the carriage around immediately for their visitor, since she "must be fatigued from her trip," and the long evening dragged to an end.

"We've just got to get a moment alone tomorrow!" whispered Ann to John as they lagged behind a bouncing Susan starting up the long stairway. As if she heard them, Susan slowed down and looked at them curiously. Ann looked helplessly at John, and he shrugged his shoulders and followed Tom to their room.

"Come on, Cousin Ann," called Susan impatiently.

Ann, her mind in a turmoil, realized the seriousness of their predicament. They might even be accused of being spies unless they left quickly. They knew too much!

5

xxxxxx

April Twelfth

Ann tried her old trick of leaving her eyes tightly closed, hoping to be able to get back into her dream if she didn't open them, but the noise was too persistent. Someone was hammering at the front door.

Reluctantly she opened one eye, and noticed an unfamiliar quilt splashed with red roses. She sat up, recalling the events of the previous day.

It wasn't a dream, she thought. I really am in Virginia, in bed with a cousin I never saw before. I'm wearing a nightgown with long sleeves and a high neck, and it's 1861, and what do I do now?

Susan was still sleeping, wrapped up in more than her share of the quilt.

The noise had stopped. Apparently someone had answered the door. She could hear the sound of excited voices and first one person and then another hurrying down the stairway.

Ann could not bear the mystery any longer. Careful not to disturb Susan, she slipped out of bed and tiptoed out into the hall.

"Oh, Lawrence, how dreadful!" Aunt Caroline sounded as if she were going to cry.

Tom appeared from the part of the hall which led to the back stairway, rubbing his eyes sleepily.

"What's the matter? Why is everybody up?" he asked.

"We have fired on Fort Sumter, Tom," his father replied gravely.

"Hurray!" Tom yelled. "Now we can shoot at those Yankees!"

"Thomas, go to your room, and never let me hear you speak like that again."

Ann thought how much she would hate to have Uncle Jefferson use that tone to her.

Tom slowly turned around and left the hall.

"I wouldn't have believed the Confederacy would go so far," Aunt Caroline said. "Whatever will happen next?"

"It all depends on how anxious the North is to fight," Uncle Lawrence replied. "It's my guess that both sides are in complete confusion."

"What will this do to William?" Aunt Caroline asked.

"I've been thinking about that all the way over here," Uncle Lawrence said slowly. "William is not completely in sympathy with either side, but he is a young man, and he is here, and a war is surely starting. Wherever his sympathies may lie, he can do nothing but enlist eventually. Already there have been some unpleasant incidents; young men he has known all his life have crossed to the other side of the street rather than speak to him."

"But, Lawrence—" Aunt Caroline's brown eyes were angry—"that's so unfair. After all, since William was five years old he has spent nearly as much time in the North as he has here. How can they expect him to turn and fight it?"

Uncle Jefferson put his arm around Aunt Caroline. "Caroline, whoever said war was fair? If this should be drawn out, as we have every reason to believe it will, hundreds, perhaps thousands, of young men like William will lose their lives."

Ann suddenly became conscious of a faint scent

of lavender, and turned to see Belle standing behind her in a long white robe, her face colorless and her hair loose around her shoulders.

As Uncle Jefferson spoke to Aunt Caroline, Belle suddenly crumpled to the floor.

Ann looked at her helplessly. She had read in books about people fainting, but she had never seen it happen before.

"Aunt Caroline, Aunt Caroline!" she called frantically.

Suddenly the hall was full of people. Aunt Caroline and the two men came running up from below, Tom and John appeared from the far end of the hall, and Susan burst out of her room, a pink robe thrown around her shoulders, and wearing only one slipper.

"Get the smelling salts on Belle's bureau," Aunt Caroline said quickly, pillowing Belle's head in her lap.

Ann rushed into Belle's room. On the bureau was a bewildering array of bottles of all shapes, colors and sizes, but none of them seemed to contain salt.

As Ann seized each bottle in turn, Susan ran into the room and grabbed a square, squat green bottle that looked as if it had perfume in it. She dashed out again, calling over her shoulder, "If it had been a snake it would have bitten you."

"Lesson one for the day," Ann said to herself. "Smelling salts aren't salt."

She was about to rejoin the people in the hall when the door opened and John slipped in cautiously.

"Listen," he said. "The first chance we have we've got to get out of here. The Confederates have fired on Fort Sumter again."

"How will we do it, John? We don't even know which way is north, or any other way for that matter. Anyway, I couldn't walk a mile in those horrible buttoned shoes."

"We'll think of something," John said, "but we need a chance to be alone."

Suddenly they could hear a confusion of voices outside the door, and John opened it for Uncle Lawrence, who was carrying Belle.

"My goodness, Ann," Aunt Caroline said disapprovingly, "you are not wearing a robe, and you're barefooted."

Ann could feel herself blushing, although, looking at the heavy nightgown with its long sleeves, she hardly felt that it was immodest. She wondered what Aunt Caroline would say about her bathing suit.

"Never mind, child," Aunt Caroline said kindly. "You were excited, of course. But get dressed quickly. Whatever the day may bring, we'll all be better off for havin' a good breakfast." She ushered Ann out of the room.

Ann did dress with unusual speed, hoping to find a chance to talk to John. Instead she met a sad-faced Aunt Caroline at the head of the stairs.

"It's a shame your first day here should be spoiled by gunfire, Ann dear," she remarked thoughtfully, "but things will look brighter to all of us after a good hot meal."

"Oh, I never eat anything for breakfast except corn flakes and orange juice," Ann replied without thinking. She hoped Aunt Caroline wasn't going to insist on oatmeal this of all mornings.

"Corn flakes?" Aunt Caroline queried. "Is that somethin' new you have in Missouri? As for orange juice, we haven't had any oranges since Christmas, but you may have strawberries or melon for your fruit."

Ann's heart sank even lower. It's too easy to

make mistakes, she thought despairingly. Corn flakes haven't even been invented yet, and they don't have oranges very often.

Now that they were in the dining room she could see the profusion of dishes holding everything from the despised oatmeal and fried corn-meal mush to pink slices of ham and a fluffy omelet.

Uncle Lawrence had joined them at the table, but he stared at his coffee as if he had no appetite and only crumbled his uneaten muffin.

Tom, however, was elated. "Now we'll show Abe Lincoln the South will fight," he crowed as he poured syrup over a stack of rice pancakes.

"It does look as if the worst has happened," said Uncle Jefferson glumly, ignoring his son's enthusiasm.

"If only those shots had not been fired," Aunt Caroline mourned.

"Mother, I do hope that old tutor won't come today," Susan said. "This is too exciting to miss. Do we have to be stuck upstairs doing sums?"

"We'll see if Mr. Tibbs comes," her mother answered. "Now run along and have Aunt Phoebe brush your hair neatly. It seems to have a mind of its own lately."

Turning to John and Ann, she became the gracious hostess they had so admired the evening before. "Now, suppose you two tell me all about your dear mother and why she insists on stayin' up in Missouri away from her family now that your father's gone."

The twins looked at each other blankly. What should they say? Fortunately, Aunt Caroline wasn't one to need much help with a conversation. Furthermore, she was obviously listening with one ear to the men, and as she probed gently for information, she was unaware of the twins' uncertainty. John and Ann managed the few phrases concerning their mother's illness that satisfied her.

"But we must have some way of finding out how much the North knows about our military situation," Uncle Lawrence said in a worried voice. "Can the Northern officers obtain accurate maps of our hills and ravines? If their scouts have already provided them with such information the South is at a disadvantage already."

Uncle Jefferson replied calmly, "It's hardly likely they have accomplished so much, but that is something to watch for—strangers interested in the lay of the land."

It seemed to Ann and John that Uncle Lawrence's gaze remained on them for an unusually long time.

It was with genuine relief that they heard the pert voice of Susan call to them to come up and see the new desks in the schoolroom, and they excused themselves hastily.

Originally built as a ballroom on the third floor, the room was now a sunny classroom for Susan and Tom, and boasted a huge fireplace and an enormous chimney which dominated one side of the room. Susan told them how satin-gowned ladies and gentlemen in brocade had danced the cotillion there.

Then Susan's interest turned to less grown-up things, and she asked John and Ann if they'd like to see her three small kittens.

The twins looked at each other and grinned. Almost together they chorused, "We love kittens and we're crazy about cats." And Ann added hopefully, "Will it take you long to get them?"

Nothing could have suited John and Ann better than to be left alone for a few precious moments, and Susan was flattered by their instant and eager response. "I'll only be gone a minute," she promised as her pink calico dress whirled through the doorway.

"Thank heavens!" John's voice was low but full of feeling. "It's about time we talked. How much more of this can you take, Ann? I'm ready to leave right now!"

"How can we get away, John?" Ann was on the verge of tears. "If we had enough money, we'd still need someone to help us. And it's too far to walk to the station, even if we could slip out."

"I wonder what other neighbors there are besides Mrs. Hurley, and how close?" John said.

"Well, there are Mr. and Mrs. Holmes—you know, the Quakers who've read *Uncle Tom's Cabin*," Ann remembered

"Good girl," John praised. "Do you suppose they might be persuaded to help us get home?"

"How could we get to them?" asked Ann.

"That's a good question. I only wish I knew the answer," John replied. "Maybe we could go out to the stables and run off with two horses. Or maybe Aunt Sarah would pack us a picnic lunch and we could say we will be gone for the day riding," he improvised.

"We've simply got to get home. If we have to

stay in this period we'll be better off in the North, because the South is going to lose the war, and we know it!"

At that exact moment the twins heard a gasp and saw telltale pink calico recede from the doorway. John rushed to the hall, but Susan had been too fast for him. The twins were certain that she had overheard at least part of a most damaging conversation.

6

XXXXXX

The Map

ANN AND John sat stiffly as they heard Susan coming back up the stairs carrying on a one-sided conversation with, they supposed, the tutor. A sharp-eyed tutor would present new difficulties, and they hoped he would be old and kindly and vague.

This hope vanished, however, when he and Susan appeared in the doorway. All Aunt Phoebe's careful work had been undone by Susan's record dash up and down the stairs. Her curls were in wild confusion, and the sash of her dress had slipped around so that the half-untied bow was almost in front. On her arm she carried a wicker basket containing three small kittens.

"These are my cousins, Ann and John," she said, at the same time waving toward the twins and trying to restrain one of the kittens from escaping from the basket. "This is Mr. Tibbs."

Mr. Tibbs gave the children a cool nod. He was a small man, with a pointed red nose which looked as if it were about to twitch. His ill-fitting black suit made him look like a disagreeable blackbird.

Tom followed Mr. Tibbs into the room, a sullen expression on his face. Without looking at Ann and John, he pointedly took a seat on the opposite side of the room.

"We thought you would probably enlist instead of coming here today," Tom said to Mr. Tibbs in a voice as close to rude as he dared make it.

"Believe me, Master Thomas," Mr. Tibbs said, doing his best not to lose his temper, "I struggled long with my conscience about that. My first impulse was to rush out in defense of our Confederacy, but more sober judgment made me realize that my real duty lay in educating the true treasure of the South—her youth."

Mr. Tibbs was so affected by his own speech that he took out a large, rather grubby handkerchief and blew his nose vigorously.

"That was very self-sacrificing of you, sir," Tom said. The trace of sarcasm in his voice echoed Ann's thoughts perfectly.

"Now then," Mr. Tibbs said, "first we must find out about our new pupils. You are from Missouri, I understand."

He said "Missouri" with considerable contempt.

"Yes," Ann said defensively.

"You had a tutor, of course."

Ann looked at John and hesitated. "Well, no," she said. "We went to a school."

"I see," said Mr. Tibbs. "Dear, dear, dear."

He tapped his teeth with a pencil. "I suppose the best thing to do would be to proceed with our lessons as usual, and give you help in the areas where you will undoubtedly need it."

"School isn't usually too hard for us," John felt it necessary to say.

"Naturally, in Missouri," sniffed Mr. Tibbs.

Suddenly Susan's kittens scrambled out of the basket and began running around the room, delighted with their new-found freedom.

"We will start with mathematics," said Mr. Tibbs, ignoring the kittens, although a gray one was toying with the idea of climbing up a leg of his trousers. "I presume you are familiar with Mason's *Problems in Algebra*?"

"No, sir," said John.

"Very well. I shall read the problems and you may copy them down. Are you ready?"

"We haven't any paper," said Ann.

"Paper?" said Mr. Tibbs haughtily. "You must have attended a very wasteful school, indeed, but I understand wastefulness to be a Yankee trait. Miss Susan, will you please provide your cousins with slates and slate pencils?"

Ann could see that John was about to explode with anger, and she looked at him and shook her head.

After Susan had brought their slates from a tall, dusty cupboard in the corner, Mr. Tibbs opened his book and read rapidly:

"Problem No. 1: A Yankee mixes a certain quantity of wooden nutmegs, which cost him one quarter cent apiece, with a quantity of real nutmegs, worth four cents apiece. The total price was $42.00, and there was a total of 4800 nutmegs. How many real nutmegs were there, and how many wooden ones did the Yankee put in?

"Problem No. 2: A Northern railroad is assessed

for $120,000 damages for contusions and broken limbs because of a collision of overcrowded cars. They were made to pay $800 for a broken limb, $400 for a major contusion, and $200 for a minor contusion. Three hundred less than 10 times the total number of contusions equals 65 times the number of broken limbs. The total number of injuries was 300. How many minor contusions were suffered because of the Yankee railroad's negligence, how many major contusions, and how many broken limbs?

"Problem No. 3: The year in which the governors of Massachusetts and Connecticut sent treasonable messages to their respective legislatures is expressed by four digits. The last two digits are equal and the second is two less than the third. If the sum of the first two digits is subtracted from the sum of the last two, the difference is 10. The sum of the digits is 26. What was this black year?"

Mr. Tibbs stopped and, noting John's angry scowl with satisfaction, asked with pretended kindness, "Am I going too fast, Master John, or do you have a question?"

"Yes, I do," John said. "I would like to ask if Mr. Mason is, perhaps, a Southern gentleman?"

Mr. Tibbs's face turned the color of his nose. "I see your school taught you to be insolent as well as wasteful, Master John, and I think I should like to speak with your aunt before further undertaking your education. While I am gone, Miss Susan, will you please remove the kittens? This is a schoolroom and not a menagerie."

He stalked from the room, followed by Tom. Susan scurried about chasing the kittens. After much crawling under desks and looking behind curtains she managed to stuff two kittens into her basket.

"Oh well," she said airily, "if I can't find the other one, Mr. I-shall-have-to-tell-your-mother Tibbs probably can't either." Susan left the room, carrying the two kittens.

There was a moment of silence broken by John, who said, "Now we're alone again, and I can't think of anything to say except 'help.' "

"I don't think Mr. Tibbs likes us much," Ann said.

"I don't think anybody likes us much," her brother agreed. "And after Susan tells them what she heard they'll be thinking we know more than we should about this war besides."

"My history teacher wouldn't think so," Ann said. "Listen, what's that noise?"

A faint rustling sound was heard from the chimney.

"It must be Susan's other kitten," John said. "Let's rescue him."

After peering up into the black inside of the chimney, John reached up and pulled out a tiny gray kitten. At the same time a small flat package wrapped in faded blue silk and tied with a black velvet ribbon fell from the chimney to his feet.

"What in the world?" they both said together. Eagerly they untied the ribbons, disclosing a neatly drawn map labeled with the names of Twinoaks and other plantations, and showing clearly the streams, woods and fields around Fairfield.

"How do you suppose that got up the chimney?" asked John.

"Up the chimney!" Ann said excitedly. "John, do you remember Aunt Hattie Lou's story about the girl who put the paper up the chimney?"

"She burned it, didn't she?" John asked.

"Maybe not, really," Ann said. "What if she somehow found a map made by the Confederates that she knew the North needed. She could have

hidden it up the chimney, and when she said it was up the chimney they would have thought she meant it was burned."

"They'd have shot her," John said.

"Not if she was Jefferson Cartwright's niece. And especially not if they couldn't find her. Remember? Aunt Hattie Lou said she disappeared."

"In any case," John said, "if, somehow in some other time this is happening again, maybe we could make it come out differently."

"You mean we could make the South win the war?"

"No, stupid. I mean that maybe if the North got the map this time they might win the first battle instead of losing it, and if they did the war might stop there."

"Ssh," Ann said, "someone's coming."

Quickly she stuffed the small package into her sash, grateful for once that she wasn't wearing shorts or blue jeans.

It was Susan. "Guess what," she said. "Mr. Tibbs isn't coming back today, but he said for you and John to study the algebra book and have the answers ready when he comes back day after tomorrow."

"Ladies first," said John gallantly, handing Ann the despised algebra book.

Ann took it and hurried to her room, trying self-consciously not to rustle. Fortunately, Susan had discovered her missing kitten and stayed behind in the schoolroom to play with it.

Quickly Ann looked around the room for a temporary hiding place. Not in her bureau drawers; she was sure Susan looked through those regularly. Not under the mattress. Aunt Phoebe would be certain to find it when she made the bed. Where would Susan never think to look?

Ann stared at the algebra book she had thrown carelessly onto her bed. Surely that would be a safe hiding place. She stuffed the blue silk and the velvet ribbon into the toe of one of her traveling boots and shut the map up beside the Yankee and his wooden nutmegs.

7

XXXXXX

The Red, White and Gray

"OH, I WISH I was in Dixie—hooray, hooray!" sang Susan and Tom loudly as the open carriage jounced down the road.

"Oh, dear! Belle, did you remember to tell Aunt Sarah to put enough salt in the potato salad?" asked Aunt Caroline as she opened the ruffled parasol which matched her dress. "Victoria Lewis is always complaining about things not being salty enough or sweet enough."

"Or too salty or too sweet," said Belle.

Ann looked at Belle's rose-sprigged dress with its yards and yards of black-velvet ribbon trimming and tried to imagine it being worn to a picnic at home. For that matter, her own thin blue dress with its wide lace-trimmed collar did not seem too appropriate either, and it certainly was neither cool nor comfortable. She smiled as she thought of Aunt Caroline's expression if she had appeared in shorts and sandals.

John's thoughts were somewhat different. He was thinking about the purpose of the picnic at the Lewis plantation. Fort Sumter had surrendered the day before, and today the American flag over the fort would have been replaced by the gray, white and red Confederate flag. John wondered if he and Ann would be able to keep their feelings from showing. Uncle Jefferson had made an excuse not to come, and John had the impression that he too felt this was not a day to be celebrated, although he did not say so.

As the carriage turned into the Lewis drive he could see that, if it weren't a joyous occasion, he and Ann were the only ones who knew it. Most of the women and girls were wearing gay ribbon cockades of the secession colors in their hair, and many of them wore the colors in sashes as well. Voices were happy, and there was much laughing and joking.

Mrs. Lewis, a tall woman with a kind but unattractive face, strode across the grass to meet them, her hat brim flopping wildly up and down.

"Caroline, my dear," she boomed in the only brisk voice they had heard since their arrival, "how nice to see you all."

She gave Ann an enthusiastic pat on the back which almost knocked her to her knees.

Aunt Caroline turned to Lafe to tell him where to place their wicker picnic hamper, but Mrs. Lewis had already taken care of it.

"Caroline, wait until you see what I've discovered," she said to Aunt Caroline in a confidential tone which Ann was sure would easily carry to the far reaches of the lawn.

Susan and Tom immediately ran to join the groups of children who were standing as close as possible to where the picnic table was being set up, and Ann and John felt relieved when Belle joined them.

"Will William be here?" Ann asked.

Belle reddened. "No," she said, "he—he had to work this afternoon."

Ann bit her tongue. Of course William wouldn't come to a party to celebrate the Confederate flag flying over an American fort, even if he were asked, which wasn't at all likely.

While she was thinking of some way to change the subject, she saw approaching them a tall girl with long dark hair, worn straight and tied back with a red ribbon. The girl was saying eagerly to Ann, "I have so much to tell you, and I can hardly wait to go ridin' with you again."

"It's nice to see you, too," said Ann, casting wildly about for some clue to her friend's identity.

Belle was unconsciously helpful. "Emily Lewis," she said, smiling, "I wondered how soon you would discover Ann was here."

As they were talking, Susan ran up to them and said, "Do come along. The grown-ups are eating already, and they're almost ready for us to start."

A long white-covered table was set up under some spreading oak trees close to the house. The huge silver platters of roast chicken and pink ham, the hot breads and dishes of vegetables would have looked more than inviting to Ann and John a few days before. But after several days of rich and elaborately served food, the twins' appetites had dwindled, and John whispered to Ann, "I'd trade the whole thing for one hamburger with onions."

"And a coke," Ann replied dreamily.

"Or a hot dog," said John.

"With mustard."

They were suddenly aware of Mrs. Lewis' voice rising above the general conversation. Seated behind an enormous silver coffee urn at one end of the table, she was saying excitedly, "We women can't carry muskets, but I do believe I have found something just as important. Now, Henry says it may not be long till all our ports are blockaded, and when they are there will be many things we will no longer have. One thing we will surely be lacking is coffee—no coffee for us and no coffee for our brave troops."

Her face lighted as she touched the coffee urn. "But here in this urn I have the answer. I have found that a very strengthening drink can be made from one third pure coffee and the rest wheat or rye, if they are roasted together so the taste of the coffee will be imparted to the grain. I assure you it is most delicious, and I implore you, ladies, to go home at once and grind this coffee and have it ready. We can store it in milk carts; we can store it in barrels; we can fill every available container until the time we need it. And now," she concluded grandly, "I want Mr. Lawrence Preston to have the first cup."

Uncle Lawrence looked a little dubious at being selected for this honor, but accepted the cup gracefully. Fortunately, Mrs. Lewis' flopping hat brim kept her from seeing the look on his face after the first sip. However, he finished the cup manfully and said gallantly, "You are right, ma'am; you have surely created a most strengthenin' drink."

Mrs. Lewis beamed as one receiving a rightful tribute, and did not seem to notice how much longer the line behind the lemonade pitcher had grown. Apparently most of the guests had suddenly noticed that it was a little warm for coffee.

After dinner the men and older boys clustered around Uncle Lawrence, eager for any news he might be able to tell them.

"What action has the North taken today?" was the question most of the men were asking.

"Lincoln has called for 75,000 volunteers," Uncle Lawrence answered gravely.

"Then we will call for 100,000," another guest asserted with confidence.

"Yes," Uncle Lawrence replied, "and soon the killing can begin in earnest."

"How soon do you think Virginia will secede?"

"Probably before the week is out," Uncle Lawrence said.

"Is it true that Colonel Robert E. Lee has been asked to resign his Army commission and head our forces?" Mr. Lewis asked.

"I don't know that he has actually been asked to resign, but there has been a good deal of speculation that he might do it."

"Robert E. Lee would never do it," said a tall dark man.

"Yes, he will," burst in John excitedly, forgetting that a twelve-year-old boy did not join in adult conversation, especially not to contradict one of his elders.

Every eye was turned toward him. He felt himself shrinking, and wished he could disappear altogether.

"Is that right, Master John?" asked Mr. Lewis sarcastically. "And what makes you so sure?"

Luckily John did not have to answer, for Uncle Lawrence said, "It's possible for anybody to hear anything in the course of a day or two."

John breathed a sigh of relief as the conversation turned back to secession.

Ann and Emily had drifted over to watch the younger children playing in a meadow beyond the carefully tended lawn. The smaller boys, and one or two of the more energetic little girls, were forming a business-like army, and Ann and Emily arrived in time to witness the swearing in. They were all lined up facing a small freckled boy.

"Raise your right hands," he said. "Say 'Glory to God, Amen.' You are now sworn in and may start fighting."

The fighting did not go too well, however, as everyone refused to be a Yankee. Emily suggested that they draw grass, the ones with the shortest pieces being Yankees. This suggestion was accepted, and they were soon going at each other with pistols and swords made out of sticks.

Having coaxed a lively pony away from one of the stable hands, Susan was the General. Some of the Yankees deserted to the Southern Army without notice, so before long the fighting was quite real in spite of Ann's and Emily's efforts at peacemaking.

Emily's little brother was the most troublesome of all. Since he was only four years old and had been included in the group only because they were playing in his meadow, he did not know one side from the other and laid wildly about him with his stick, whacking Confederate and Yankee shins alike.

"Private Lewis," Susan said severely, "I am afraid I will have to have you put in the guard-house."

Private Lewis picked up a stone and shied it angrily at Susan, screaming, "There, you old General, you."

The stone grazed the foreleg of Susan's pony, which reared back and then bolted toward the road. Susan rode well, but the pony was terror-stricken and doing its best to unseat her. As she disappeared from sight, she had lost the reins and was clinging to the pony's neck, slipping first to one side and then to the other.

Almost immediately the meadow filled with the older guests, who had heard the children's horrified screams.

"She's such a little girl," Belle said to Ann. "Why didn't we watch her?" She was sobbing.

"Please don't worry, Belle," Ann comforted her. "Lafe will rescue her."

As if she were watching a scene in a play, Ann

saw Lafe come running up carrying a much subdued Susan. Fortunately the pony had run past the slave quarters where Lafe was visting his sister. The pony had slowed down a little and Lafe had been able to grab its bridle and calm it.

Susan was unhurt, and was soon enjoying her promotion from general to queen. It was a great satisfaction all around to see Private Lewis being led off for a spanking.

On the way home Belle turned to Ann and said, "Ann, however could you know that Lafe would rescue Susan? We didn't know where the pony went or where Lafe was, either."

"Aunt Hattie Lou told me," Ann answered absently.

"Who?" asked Belle and Tom in chorus.

"That's Ann's way of saying she made a good guess," John explained.

"How very odd," Aunt Caroline said. "You know, Hattie Lou is a name in your Uncle Jefferson's family." Aunt Caroline proceeded happily with the genealogy of all the Hattie Lou's in the family, while Ann determined to hold her tongue the next time one of Aunt Hattie Lou's stories came to mind.

8

XXXXXX

Of Needling and Needles

AN UNSEEN honeybee outside the church window hummed drowsily in the hot June sunshine. A warm breeze moved the masses of honeysuckle lazily along the sill. Mesmerized by the gentle stirring of the secession ribbons on the bonnet of the woman in the pew ahead, Ann's eyes closed. In spite of her fear that the minister would notice, her head nodded.

As John's elbow found her ribs, the Reverend Morgan suddenly barked out a rousing call to arms for all patriotic citizens of the South. Ann demurely smoothed out a wrinkle in her dainty blue dimity dress, hoping no one had seen her jump.

What a thunderous voice he had! There could be no nodding in a church with a minister as militant as this. Both the twins had been surprised to hear opinions expressed so forcibly from the pulpit.

This was no middle-of-the-road sermon. This minister was as violently partisan as his congregation. He reminded his charges that their slaves were utterly dependent on their masters for their livelihood, and that defense of slavery must be considered a repetition of the revolution of 1776.

"And it does appear that nothing will stop our Yankee brethren from fighting," he concluded.

John felt beads of perspiration popping out on his forehead as he recalled the recent secession of Tennessee from the Union and wondered if Ann was remembering Uncle Lawrence's prediction that there would soon be a battle near by.

To the twins' relief, the sermon finally came to a close, and the congregation stood to sing the closing hymn.

William's clear tenor rang out in the stanzas of "Awake, My Soul, Stretch Every Nerve." It took real courage for him to face the curt nods from hostile patriots this morning, Ann thought.

Outside on the grass of the churchyard, small

groups gathered, talking heatedly, praising General Lee for resigning his commission in the United States Army to head the Confederate Army, speculating optimistically about the probable length of the war. The children, too, chattered with more excitement than their usual Sunday decorum permitted. Even the horses, some saddled and some harnessed to carriages, moved restlessly.

John and Ann were all too aware of the mounting tension. As they passed by Mrs. Hurley, she stopped abruptly in the middle of a conversation to ask irritatingly in her nasal tones, "Ann, didn't the sermon interest you? I couldn't rightly nap through a rousin' speech like that!" Fortunately, Ann didn't have to reply as Belle strolled over to her and stanchly championed the twins by placing her arm around Ann's shoulder.

When they were out of earshot, Ann inquired, "Did I snore or something, John?"

John looked serious as he answered, "No, it isn't you; it's both of us. Let's face it, Ann, we're Yankees and we're not among friends here."

"Cousin John," Belle tried to console him, "you're our family, and Cartwrights all stick together."

"Looks more like you're stuck with us," John tried to joke.

Tom sauntered up, looking pleased with himself. "The Reverend Morgan was speaking right to you two this morning," he chortled.

John held onto his temper with difficulty. "Now is the time for all good men to come to the aid of their country," he quipped.

Ann glanced at him with understanding. She knew exactly how he felt—worried inside, but all bravado outside.

"Well, show you're a good man, then," Tom countered. "Forget you're a Yankee."

John's fists tightened, but before he could answer, Belle's soft voice spoke with unaccustomed firmness, "Thomas Cartwright! If Father heard you, you know what he would do. And on Sunday, too!"

Tom glowered sulkily. "I made sure he couldn't hear," he boasted, glancing over at the church where Jefferson Cartwright was still talking to the minister.

He's probably inviting him to dinner, Ann thought resignedly. Oh, this wasn't fun, being so far from home in both geography and time! So many things had happened—would happen—in April of this year, and Ann wished desperately for her all-too-often-neglected history book.

A laugh startled Ann back to reality as Mrs. Lewis marched up to the group of young people.

"You all look as if the battle's already begun right here," Mrs. Lewis said. As Tom and John continued to scowl at each other, she nodded at them. "I know what you need," she told them. "Another picnic!" And she charged off to organize a group of women to knit socks for the Army.

"Wow," muttered John, "I was afraid she was going to say we needed some of her coffee." And turning his back on Tom he wandered off in the direction of the horses. At least *they* wouldn't blame him for being born on the wrong side of the map.

As he passed a group of neighbors, he heard Mr. Lewis complaining, "But they said the Army will be confiscating horses next. I can't rightly part with mine just now."

"Who are 'they'?" asked Uncle Lawrence.

"Oh, I don't remember their names, but they said even boys of fourteen would soon be fighting."

Uncle Lawrence laughed good-naturedly.

"Henry Lewis, if you ever find out the names of 'them,' I'll be glad to write that story and put it on the front page of my paper. I wish I had a dollar for every rumor I've heard about what 'they' said."

Mr. Lewis grinned and turned away, but John winced. No wonder there was so much confusion on both sides when there was a rumor for every fear.

Just then Uncle Jefferson motioned for Lafe to bring the carriage, and as if she had been waiting for this, Mrs. Hurley joined them. "I was just sure to goodness Bucky was coming for me, but I don't see that slowpoke yet. You wouldn't mind carrying me home, would you?"

"Carry?" Ann gasped, picturing the strong-willed Mrs. Hurley cradled in Uncle Jefferson's arms.

" 'Carry' as in 'Carry Me Back to Ole Virginny,' " John whispered, moving closer to Ann. "Maybe 'they' have confiscated her horses already!"

Uncle Jefferson, gallant as always, assisted the lady into the carriage and replied, "We'd be mighty happy to have you stay for dinner, too, especially since the Reverend Morgan is coming for the afternoon."

"What a patriotic meal this should be!" commented Ann softly. "I just wish I didn't know how the War Between the States turned out. They're so thrilled over the twentieth of May."

"What happened then?" John inquired.

Ann looked at him quizzically. "Don't you remember three weeks ago when North Carolina seceded and the next day Richmond was selected as the capital of the Confederacy?"

"Oh, yes," John agreed quickly. Then, noticing the few people left in the churchyard, he suggested, "Let's hurry to catch up with the family or we'll be left all alone here."

"That idea has possibilities," Ann muttered, "though I can hardly wait to change from all these petticoats into something comfortable."

"You can't, Ann," John protested. "There's company today."

"Today and every day," Ann mourned. "But nothing in that clothes press is comfortable anyway. Doesn't it seem strange not to have any closets?"

"Very strange," John agreed. "Ann, let's ask if we may walk home. The carriage is so crowded, and we've got some planning to do. There are just too many people around us all the time."

"Wel-ll," Ann reluctantly approved the idea. Her kid slippers had not been made for hiking.

But just as they thought they would have some time alone, Bucky drove up and Mrs. Hurley suggested that all the children ride with him. Surprisingly, the drive was a happy one, for Tom started imitating Mrs. Lewis' vigorous speech in such a way that even Bucky's broad shoulders were soon shaking with laughter. So it seemed only a short time until Bucky drove up to the piazza with a flourish, and the children hurried into the cool, high-ceilinged house to get ready for dinner.

The afternoon passed quickly enough, though John was glad to escape to the stables with Tom after the dinner-table talk of Mrs. Hurley and the Reverend Morgan. Those two thought alike and aloud, and Uncle Jefferson found it difficult to maintain a calm suitable to Sunday.

After dinner, the men retired to the library to smoke and talk while the women and girls sat on the wide veranda fragrant with wisteria, knitting stockings for the soldiers.

"This is something my mother would have taken a stick to me for doing on a Sunday," said Mrs. Hurley, and her chair rocked jerkily for a moment.

"Everyone knits on Sunday now," Belle assured her, "and some ministers even permit it in church."

"That's going a bit too far." Aunt Caroline's rocker moved smoothly as her busy fingers turned a heel.

Ann was doing her best to remain inconspicuous as she sat on one of the steps half hidden by pink azaleas. She had never knitted before and so far had not learned to handle the three sock needles with any degree of skill. All too soon she heard Susan complain, "It's not fair, Mother, for Ann not to knit if I have to."

Aunt Caroline's tone was gently reproving. "Ann, dear, if you keep trying, you'll soon learn. We all make mistakes at first."

"I can't imagine a well-brought-up young lady not knowing how to knit," said Mrs. Hurley, raising her eyebrows at Ann.

"It looks so simple when you do it," Ann replied, "but even cellophane tape wouldn't keep my stitches from falling off."

Susan giggled. "You say the silliest things. You mean you drop your stitches."

"What's cellophane tape?" Mrs. Hurley's quick ear had noticed the unfamiliar phrase.

"Oh, it's—" Ann stopped, then continued uneasily. "It's a very useful sticky ribbon that Mother says she couldn't keep house without. I'll have her send you some when I get home." *If* I ever get home, she thought.

"I can't imagine a sticky ribbon helping you knit this woolly yarn."

"I just wish I could show you how useful it can be, ma'am," Ann answered truthfully. Then, turning to Belle, she said, "I'd appreciate it if you'd strike some stitches on for me again."

"Strike? Oh, you mean cast on. Yes, I'll be glad to. Give me your needles and yarn, honey."

"I knew it had something to do with fishing," Ann laughed. "My knitting bag's in my room. I'll go up and get it." And she jumped to her feet quickly, grateful for the opportunity to move about. As she raced up the stairs two at a time, she was glad there was no one watching her to comment on the behavior of young ladies.

In her room, Ann found Aunt Phoebe straightening up Susan's hat, mitts and handkerchief where they had been tossed in a heap.

"She's a real untidy child," Aunt Phoebe said, laughing, "but she do brighten up this old house."

"You're very fond of this family, aren't you?" Ann asked.

"I've never known any other," Aunt Phoebe replied, "and I ain't fixin' to find any other, either. I'm satisfied right here."

"Are most of the other slaves happy, too?" Ann asked.

"They are around here, Miss Ann, but over at Mrs. Hurley's, things ain't so good. Bucky told Lafe about how they're mighty restless over there."

"Would they dare to run away?" whispered Ann.

"Maybe things are no better where they run to, Miss Ann," and the loyal slave lowered her voice, too. "This a'ways, they get their food and clothes regular, and medicine too when they sick. If they run off, how they going to find someone to take care of them up North? They just get caught, and lawsy me! They get a whippin' then! But hush, child, Mister Jefferson skin me alive if he hear you talkin' like this to old Phoebe."

At this thought, Aunt Phoebe glanced at the door, and her brown eyes widened in horror. Mrs. Hurley was standing stiffly in the doorway, an accusing frown on her face.

"Maybe he should be told that his Northern

visitor is incitin' our slaves to run away." Mrs. Hurley's tone was cold.

"Oh, no, ma'am! I wouldn't do that!" Ann felt her cheeks burning with indignation.

"Well, being an impulsive Northerner, maybe you didn't rightly realize that slavery's no subject of conversation for a child. I'd say it's high time for you twins to be goin' home if you're beginnin' to be troublemakers without even trying."

Ann listened with downcast eyes, her attitude respectful, her emotions furious. How she wished they could go home!

"Now, miss, you go right along downstairs and I'll get the quilt blocks I left here last week," Mrs. Hurley concluded her lecture.

Ann stumbled along the hall, almost forgetting the knitting needles in her distress. Of all times for that woman to be an eavesdropper. What would John say? More important, what would Uncle Jefferson say if Mrs. Hurley told him?

Ann was an unhappy girl as she joined the others on the piazza and prepared to concentrate on knitting one and purling one.

9

XXXXXX

The Underground Railway

THE NOISE wasn't loud, but it was persistent. It sounded like pebbles pelting against the bedroom window. The room was quite dark.

John, who hadn't slept very well because of the plans for escape that he had been making and rejecting, almost woke Tom to help him investigate. Later, he shuddered at the thought of what might have happened if Tom had roused.

Although the rest of the family still treated the twins as usual, Tom had become more and more hostile as tension mounted in the South.

But there was that sound again!

Rolling awkwardly out of the soft, high bed,

John padded noiselessly to the white-curtained window. It was open and he could hear the hoarse breathing of someone who had been running hard.

"Who's there?" John whispered.

Without a moment's hesitation, a soft voice answered, "A friend with friends."

John's heart skipped a beat. Aunt Hattie Lou had told them that was one of the passwords for the slaves traveling the Underground Railway! He knew it wasn't a real train, but a series of homes owned by sympathizers of the slaves. She had told them also about the many long years it had been in existence before the war, and about how the runaway slaves had been hidden or helped on to the next "station."

But this was all wrong! There was certainly no one at Twinoaks who was in the least sympathetic with valuable slave property running away to the North. It was providential that he and not Tom had heard the pebbles.

John whispered guardedly, "Stay in the shadows until I can come out to you, and don't make any noise."

Whoever it was must be intelligent, John decided, for there was no answer.

As quietly as possible, John tiptoed across the dark room only to crash into the little rocking chair he had forgotten. Luckily Tom was in a deep sleep, and although he turned over, muttering that it was too early to get up, he soon was snoring evenly again. John rubbed his aching ankle and started cautiously for the door once more.

If I just had my flashlight, he thought. This is worse than the inside of a balloon!

The door, although solid, was noisy, and it creaked and squealed until John was positive the entire household must be alarmed. But as he slid slowly around and out into the hall, he heard no alarm given.

"Now to deal with that stairway," John sighed. "It may look romantic with pretty girls in wide skirts gliding down it, but with no lights it's strictly a traffic hazard."

He worried for fear the escaping slave would try to arouse someone else if he didn't appear soon, and yet if he hurried and upset the hand-painted umbrella stand by the door, he'd have more help than he needed.

Finally the doorknob was in his hand, and he began to breathe more easily as he stepped out onto the porch. Jester, the spaniel, began to bark loudly, and John collapsed weakly against the railing. Then he remembered with relief that no one paid any attention to Jester's barking.

As he moved down the steps to the lawn, a darker shadow slid quietly out from the huge mass of lilac bushes. The flashing white teeth of a tall, good-looking Negro made John smile in spite of himself—a walking toothpaste ad, he couldn't help thinking. In the right century, this man might have earned his living just by grinning for a photographer.

"Oh, sir, I'm right glad to see you!" And the big, muscular figure came up close. Attempting to quiet the man, John drew the slave farther away from the house into the denser foliage of the magnolia trees and tried to figure out a hiding place. He realized the need for speed, but rejected the nearby stables as being too risky.

John listened to the recital of woes that had beset the Negro—Big Sam—after the death of his beloved "Ol' Massa."

It was a common story. As the young son took over the management of the plantation, the slaves became property rather than individuals, the kindly overseer was replaced, working hours were increased, families were divided, and the cotton fields witnessed many cruel whippings. When Big Sam's young daughter was sold away from the plantation, he and his wife decided to join the scores of others running away successfully to the North, helped by the Underground Railway.

Not until then did John listen with undivided attention. "You're not alone?" he gasped.

"No, sir, my wife, Becky, came along with me." For the first time doubt crept into his intelligent face. "You won't fail us now, will you? We've walked ever so far, and we're so tired," he pleaded.

Now John was really frightened. One was bad enough to hide—but two! How could he supply two with adequate food? His mind raced, then skidded to a stop as he heard Big Sam say, "They told us we'd find friends on the road out of Fairfield."

John relaxed a trifle. Probably Ben Holmes kept a station for the Underground Railway, as many of the Quakers did, and the man had merely come to the wrong red brick house. Well—if it was just for one night, maybe there was a chance to get away with it. He felt like a character in a cloak-and-dagger drama. John thought, All I need now is a mask and cape.

It was probably about midnight, he judged, and he'd have to be back in bed before Tom missed him.

Desperately, he began to improvise. "All right, Big Sam, of course I'll help you both. Get your wife and hide far back of the house in the wooded ravine all day. There's a clear creek there and you'll have water to drink. I'll try to bring something for you to eat and leave it under the rose bushes. Listen for my owl's hoot by the two big oak trees behind the stables, but wait a long time before you come out. Tonight I'll try to sneak out again to tell you where to go to find the station. I can't help you more than that, but the Quakers down the road will. Come back to the stables after dark and wait for me. Just don't be afraid, and don't move around."

I'd better take my own advice, John thought grimly as he turned toward the huge brick house and watched Big Sam, followed by a smaller shadow, cross from the shade made by the mimosas to that of the magnolias.

Why didn't I ask him if he thought he was being followed? he reproached himself. Big Sam had been on the road almost three weeks, long enough to be missed and a description circulated in the papers. Uncle Lawrence's newspaper ran a column of ads about escapees, and it made the twins miserable to read it. Most slaves preferred to be killed rather than captured.

"Ann and I will have to pretend to eat ravenously and put our food in our napkins," John decided. "If they see us, maybe they'll think it's just Yankee manners. Tonight I'll have to make Tom believe I'm asleep, then slip out later to take them food and the directions to the Holmes house—which I don't even know myself."

He could hardly wait to tell Ann that he had recruited two passengers for the Underground Railway.

As he quietly re-entered the house, he glanced back along the peaceful, wide lawn, the winding drive, and the shadowy bushes. Gratefully, he noticed there was no movement of any kind. Jester lay panting on the porch, unaware of the anxious look John shot in his direction.

Aside from the ominous creaking of the second step as he started up the long stairway, John reached his room safely.

He wasn't in the least surprised to see Ann waiting outside Tom's door for him. Somehow she always sensed when he was in trouble.

"I woke up worrying about you and then I heard you bump into something," she whispered. "Were you figuring on escaping without me?"

John grinned. "Not exactly," he said. "I was trying to help two slaves escape."

"Oh, John, really!"

"Honestly, Ann, there are two slaves out back in the ravine hunting for the Underground Railway."

He described the events of the evening. "Tomorrow, let's save what food we can stuff into my pockets and your sash, and hope we can get out to the stables to look at the horses. If we have any luck, we can get the food to them."

A noise from Tom's room made him pause and look warningly at Ann. Without another word, the twins turned to tiptoe back to bed.

10

XXXXXX

Quaker Hospitality

ONLY THE thought of Uncle Jefferson's face if a straggler appeared at breakfast kept John from pulling the covers over his head again when Aunt Caroline tapped at their door in the morning. He had lain awake until almost daybreak listening to Tom's heavy breathing and thinking about Big Sam and Becky and Mr. Holmes.

"Did you all sleep well?" Aunt Caroline asked, as usual, at the breakfast table.

Tom said crossly, "No, I hardly slept at all."

John looked at him skeptically, but, happy that Aunt Caroline had not noticed he was tired, said nothing.

"I didn't either," Susan said. "I woke up, and I was sure I heard somebody walking out in the hall, and I heard that second stair squeak."

Aunt Caroline shook her head. "Susan, if that stair squeaked as often as you hear it in the night it would be purely worn out by now."

At this point they heard voices in the hall, and Uncle Lawrence came in. He often visited them in the morning. He looked as if he had not slept well either.

"Am I too late for breakfast?" he asked. "I didn't go home from the office at all last night. It seems certain now that the western part of the state will take its oath of loyalty to the Union today."

"How could they?" Tom asked. "They're just as much Southern as we are."

"It's over the issue of slavery," his father explained. "And, Tom, they have as much right to stay with the Union as Virginia had to leave it, if Virginia did have the right to leave the Union."

"Why do I have to live in the only house in the South where everybody is always seeing both sides of everything?" Tom asked despairingly. "Everywhere else people think the war is glorious."

"Glorious!" Uncle Jefferson said contemptuously. "It's easy to enjoy a war with no casualties, no wounded, no mourning anywhere—all flags and speeches and marching. But that happy kind of war is about over, and the North will be bound to take action soon, quite possibly near here."

Tom tried not to look elated at the thought of a battle in his own back yard.

"The talk is," Uncle Lawrence said, "that now everyone will be required to send all available slaves to build a breastworks at Fairfield. Of course this country is an ideal spot in which to defend ourselves, because the Northern generals probably have no idea of the number of hills and ravines here. At least we're reasonably sure they do not."

Ann almost stopped breathing, thinking about the map she had hidden. This time the map must go to President Lincoln, she thought desperately.

Looking at John, she saw that he was trying to transfer a piece of ham from his plate to his handkerchief.

"Aunt Caroline," she wailed loudly, "how will we ever get home now?" She even managed a few tears; after all, she really did want to go home. As she pulled her handkerchief out of her sash she managed to tip over her glass of milk, and was pleased to note out of the corner of her eye that during the mopping up process John added several sausages from the platter to his collection.

"Oh, Lawrence," Aunt Caroline said, patting Ann's hand absent-mindedly, "will things ever be the way they were again?"

Uncle Lawrence smiled at her sadly. "Well, Caroline," he said, "even in the midst of all this you hear funny things. This morning Roger Bradley repeated a story his father used to tell about conscripting during the War of 1812. As the line passed by the recruiting officer everyone was supposed to say if there was any reason he could not be in the Army. One man said one of his legs was too short, and was dismissed. The man just behind him decided to be safer yet, and said both his legs were too short."

John laughed at this more than was necessary, and somehow his fork clattered to the floor. Ann seized the opportunity to slip three hotcakes from a plate which was being passed, and to stuff them into her sash.

Uncle Jefferson looked at John with displeasure and suggested that he and Uncle Lawrence retire to his study where it was quieter.

Aunt Caroline said, "Let me bring you a plate of hot breakfast, Lawrence. You still haven't eaten anything. No one has."

"John has," Tom said spitefully. "He's eaten nearly all the sausages."

His mother frowned at him. "Thomas, we do not usually count how many sausages our guests eat. When I come back I want to find you getting along nicely as cousins should."

Left alone, the children stared at one another in uncomfortable silence.

Then Tom said suddenly, "Don't think I don't know you want the North to win, but they won't. Anyone knows one Southerner can lick any dozen Yankees."

"It isn't particularly what I want or don't want," John said, "but after all there are only half as many people in the South. We—I mean the North—have an army already trained, and all the factories to make equipment. And we've got Abraham Lincoln."

"Abraham Lincoln," snorted Tom. "A big help he'll be!"

"Abraham Lincoln!" Ann exclaimed, her eyes blazing. "Abraham Lincoln was the greatest man who ever lived. How dare you talk that way?"

"Was the greatest man?" Tom said. "Did something happen to him? What do you know?"

"They know lots," Susan said. "Why, John said——"

Realizing that Susan was about to tell what she had overheard in the schoolroom, Ann jumped up, determined to create some sort of a diversion.

At that moment Aunt Caroline appeared in the doorway, and one of the hotcakes fell out of Ann's sash to the floor. They all stared at it for a moment, hypnotized. Ann could see Aunt Caroline deciding what course of action to take.

"Ann, dear," she said finally, "if you feel that you did not have enough breakfast to last until dinnertime you are quite free to go to the kitchen and ask Aunt Sarah for something. I am afraid hotcakes might make your sash greasy. I declare, you're all actin' most peculiarly," she added with a sigh.

Ann decided it was better to be thought greedy than to attempt an explanation, and remained silent. It was a wise decision, for Aunt Caroline apparently thought it best to let the matter drop. She said, "I heard Mrs. Holmes is feelin' poorly, since her fall. I'll go out to fix a basket and you can all ride down and take it to her." Shaking her head, she picked up the hotcake and went to the kitchen.

"I don't want to take Ben Holmes a basket," Tom muttered under his breath so there would be no danger of his mother overhearing. "Some people think they're helping slaves to escape, and I believe it. I've heard wagons going toward there lots of times in the night, and why should they be going there for any good reason?"

"Quakers do what they think is right," John said, "and they don't think it's right for one person to own another person."

"I don't think it's right for one person to steal another person's property," Tom said belligerently.

Aunt Caroline came back with a small wicker basket covered with a white fringed napkin. "And I don't think it's right for cousins to quarrel all the time. Run along upstairs and put on your riding clothes," she said, pushing them toward the door.

John felt a surge of hope for their plans and knew without looking at Ann that she was as thrilled as he was.

Ann and John followed their cousin up the stairway. Clearly Tom was not going to forget easily that a Southern home sheltered Yankees. However, this time John was glad of Tom's dislike, for, picking up his crop, Tom dashed down to the stables and left him alone in the room.

John wrapped his morning's loot in a clean towel and quickly wrote a note to the unknown Holmes family, telling them that two slaves would come to their house that night if all went well.

He hoped to conceal the food under the rose bushes while the horses were being readied, and to hide the note in the basket for the Holmes. He wondered if he should attempt a note to the slaves, but decided against it, remembering that usually only the house slaves were taught to read.

Hearing Aunt Caroline call, "Susan, please come downstairs for a moment," and Susan's skipping footsteps on the stairs, John quickly left his room, hoping to have a few words with Ann.

Ann was already on her way to meet him, awkward in her riding skirt, but as anxious as he to make use of every moment they were together.

"There are two pancakes and three biscuits in this napkin," she told him, tucking it out of sight. "With your ham and sausages, we did quite well, don't you think?"

"Yes, for Big Sam," whispered John in reply, "but not so well for ourselves. I could hardly keep from laughing, Uncle Jefferson looked so disgusted as we dropped forks and spilled milk. Maybe he'll be glad to send us back home if we annoy him enough, though he does try hard to be nice to us."

"If only we could think of a plan of escape," Ann mourned. "Every hour brings the War Between the States closer."

"Yes," John replied gloomily, "Fairfield is too close to Bull Run and Manassas. Haven't you heard Uncle Lawrence talking about the picket lines and breastworks the Confederate Army is setting up near Mrs. Hurley's plantation?"

"Picket lines?" Ann was horrified and her voice rose, arousing Belle.

"Whatever is the matter, you two?" she inquired, opening the door of her room.

Ann's concern was genuine. "Oh, I can't tell you how sorry we are to have bothered you," she apologized.

Belle's eyes were swollen, but she spoke gently. "I heard what you said, Ann." Not hearing Ann's gasp of dismay, she went on, "Of course we're all worried about picket lines and the possibility of a battle close by, but I'm sure our Southern soldiers will keep us safe, so don't you children worry your heads about it." And she returned to her room.

"Bet she's worrying plenty about William," John guessed.

"He'll have to fight with the South, won't he?"

"Not if he can leave it and go back to his grandparents in New York," John replied slowly, and the twins looked at each other as an idea came to both at the same time.

"Ann! John! Come on down to the stables. I'm not going to wait any longer for you." Susan's impatient voice floated up the stairway. "You bring the basket. Mother's waitin' for an apple pie to come out of the oven."

"What luck!" whispered John as Ann answered, "Coming!"

At the stables an opportunity was offered them to carry out their plans. Satin Lady, the favorite riding horse and pet of the family, had had a new foal that night. Tom and Susan were hanging over her stall bars admiring the new arrival with noisy enthusiasm, so that no one noticed the three clear owl hoots John voiced or the quick hiding of Ann's parcel under the rose bushes.

John had also been able to tuck his letter out of sight in the Holmes basket, but the spicy aroma of the still-warm apple pie was too much for him. Hastily, he removed it and transferred it to the rose bushes too, while Ann nervously watched the stable entrance.

As they rejoined the admiring group around the wobbly, fuzzy black colt, the twins exchanged a look of relief. This time they had been lucky. How long would their luck continue?

Their horses were saddled and waiting, so the children mounted and Tom and Susan led them down the curving road at a brisk canter. For once, conversation was not necessary, and John concentrated on remembering the roads they crossed as they neared the neat red brick house of Ben Holmes.

It wasn't far. John decided that if Big Sam cut across a field instead of following the road, it might be safer. However, it would depend upon the weather. The bright morning sun had been hidden by soft gray clouds, and a cool breeze was blowing Susan's curls into their usual tangle.

The twins were relaxed and happy for the first time since the bumpy little train had deposited

them in the midst of a strange century. John and Ann genuinely loved horseback riding, and these horses were thoroughbreds in every sense of the word.

Ben Holmes, a sturdy, calm-looking man, came to the door as they dismounted and greeted them cordially, expressing pleasure at seeing John and Ann again. As Tom handed the basket to Mr. Holmes, John could hardly breathe for fear he would see the note and take it out too soon, but that crisis passed safely.

Another crisis arose, however, as Mrs. Holmes.

seated in the parlor, her ankle swathed in a blanket, raised the fringed napkin and exclaimed at the calf's-foot jelly and fragrant fruit cake. Susan, curious as ever, peeked in too, and remarked, "What happened to the apple pie Mother was goin' to put in, Ann?"

Ann quickly improvised, "Oh, she told me it was still too warm to send," and hoped Susan would forget to check on this piece of information.

Tom was behaving in a most peculiar manner, walking around the walls of the small room and obviously listening for something. His host ignored him for a while and then asked quietly, "Is there something thee wishes, Tom?"

Although Tom had the grace to blush, his voice was curt as he replied, "Nothing I can ask for yet."

Susan's mouth dropped open. What had become of Tom's usual good manners? Since John and Ann had come, he had become so cross and surly.

John and Ann knew Tom was hoping to discover a sliding panel by the fireplace, or a cupboard over a warming oven where an escaping slave could hide. He was listening for voices behind the walls, or strange noises made by runaway slaves concealed in hidden storage rooms. Mrs. Holmes chatted on to Ann as if to cover Tom's rude remark.

"Thee has grown so tall since last year. When this ankle permits me to walk again, thee must ride over again for some ginger cookies. Thee used to like them, Ann."

"Oh, I still do, ma'am," Ann heard herself answer and glanced at John, knowing he also was wondering if they themselves could expect help from this quarter. But then, after all, the Holmeses couldn't be expected to assist a neighbor's guests, and children at that, to run away.

John was hoping to talk to Mr. Holmes alone, but Tom showed no inclination to leave him, and after a brief conversation the four said good-by, promising to return soon.

All the way home, John wondered if he had made a mistake in writing his note. Could this normal, serene home really be a station of the Underground Railway?

Just as they rode into the stableyard the first drops of rain began to fall, and John grimaced. He hoped rain wouldn't complicate tonight's adventure; it would be tricky enough without damp clothes to explain.

11

Of Rain and Runaways

IT SEEMED as if the evening would never end. Aunt Caroline, still trying to awaken some friendship between the two boys, suggested a taffy pull after dinner, an idea which Susan enthusiastically seconded. Aunt Sarah was somewhat less enthusiastic, but she stirred up the syrup in a big iron kettle, and Belle supervised the pulling. Ann and John burned their fingers and were not too happy with the sticky, gray product they produced, but Susan and Tom seemed to enjoy it.

Just as they were cutting the taffy into pieces they heard a loud clap of thunder, and sheets of water began to beat against the kitchen windows.

Susan ran to Belle and buried her face in her apron.

Belle said, "Let's go into the parlor and sing. I remember what a pretty voice Ann has, and that way we won't hear the rain."

John looked desperately at the grandfather clock in the hall. It was almost nine o'clock. Usually Aunt Caroline insisted that they go to bed at eight-thirty, but tonight she hadn't even sent Susan upstairs.

Belle sat down at the huge square rosewood piano. "Do you know 'Old Black Joe?' " she asked.

"Oh, yes," Ann said eagerly. "That's one of the songs Daddy used to sing to us when we were little."

Belle laughed. "I don't think so, honey. 'Old Black Joe' was just written last year."

Ann bit her lip. "I guess I wasn't remembering right," she said. "This 'Old Black Joe' must be one I don't know."

They sang and they sang and they sang. John yawned noisily, hoping Aunt Caroline would notice and say that it was time for bed, but she sat quietly smiling over her knitting and tapping her feet to the music.

"I declare," Belle said, "this music makes you forget all about the storm. I like a stormy night when everyone is safe and dry at home."

John thought about Big Sam and Becky, huddled together somewhere in the ravine, wet and terrified and miserable.

At last Aunt Caroline rolled up her knitting and said, "I'm sure we've all enjoyed the music, but now it's well past everyone's bedtime."

Ann was as eager to go to bed as John. Somehow she had an uneasy feeling that she should check on the map. She never had moved it from its hiding place. Since Mr. Tibbs no longer came, the algebra was not used by anyone, and it seemed as good a place of concealment as any in this household, where privacy was not easily come by.

As soon as she entered the bedroom she looked toward the top of the bureau for reassurance, but the familiar thin brown book was gone.

Susan had just pulled her nightgown over her head.

"Susan," Ann said, trying not to sound excited, "have you seen the algebra book?"

"What in the world do you want with an algebra book this time of night?" Susan asked sleepily.

"Oh, nothing," Ann said casually. "I just thought I might work out some problems in the morning."

"Well," Susan said, yawning, "Tom had the same idea. He came in before supper and got it."

Ann's heart sank. Tom, of all people. Could there be any way to get the book back before he opened it?

She didn't know whether to worry more about the map or about John trying to go out in the storm.

John was beset by his own difficulties. Ordinarily Tom was asleep by the time John got into bed, but tonight he was disposed to stay awake and argue about states' rights and slavery and Abraham Lincoln. At last John managed to end the conversation by pretending to be asleep, and he soon heard the reassuring sound of Tom's heavy breathing on the other side of the bed.

"My kingdom for a pair of rubber boots," John thought, as he pulled on his clothes in the dark.

This time he remembered to avoid the rocking chair, and not to step on the second stair. However, as he neared the doorway, he crashed into the umbrella stand, sending umbrellas clattering in every direction. Unnerved, he began crawling on his hands and knees toward the dining room.

Suddenly a shaggy black shape appeared before him. John thought of haunted houses, and then he realized that the shape was Jester, who had been sleeping under the dining room table.

"Jester, you crazy dog," John whispered. "Please, please don't bark."

But Jester was happy to have found a companion under the table, and was licking his face wetly. John sat there for what seemed an eternity, but apparently the noise had been attributed to the storm. Cautiously he crawled back into the hall, trying to foresee any other likely booby traps. Jester bounded along joyously beside him, happy with this delightful new game.

As John opened the heavy front door, torrents of rain beat against him, and only the thought of Sam and Becky made him walk away from the warm, dry house. Jester sensibly refused to step off the veranda.

It was hard to find his way to the ravine in the complete blackness, but after what seemed like hours of miserable, wet walking he came to the two big oaks.

"They'll never hear me whistle," he thought tiredly, but before he had an opportunity to try he saw Sam's flashing teeth, and realized that both slaves were huddled as close to the tree as they could get. It gave them at least a feeling of shelter.

"I told Becky that boy would be here somehow, someway," Sam said through chattering teeth.

"Now listen," John said, "I can't be gone much longer, but you go back to the road you came on and keep going until you come to the next red brick house. They'll be expecting you."

"Oh," wailed Becky, "please, please, sir, don't leave us to find our way alone. Sam's so tired and muddled he'd never find it, and they'll pick us up an' have us sent back, and this time Marse'll kill us sure."

"All right," John said, hoping they could not tell that he was as frightened as they were.

Slowly they made their way back to the road, and as they reached it the rain began to slacken a little. Nevertheless, the short journey had been enough for them to become thoroughly soaked.

A light was showing at the rear of the Holmes house. Apparently they were expected. Was that good or bad? John wondered. His heart beat so fast he forgot to think about his wet feet. The house loomed larger and larger.

Suddenly John stopped still. Was it his imagination, or did he really hear a horse galloping down the road?

The noise grew louder. It wasn't his imagination. What did they do with people who helped slaves escape—shoot them or hang them?

"Down," he croaked excitedly, but Sam and Becky, more accustomed to sudden alarms, were already lying flat on their faces at the side of the road.

The solitary rider was within hailing distance now.

"Stop," he called, "who is it?"

Hopelessly John turned around to face William.

"John Cartwright," William said, "what are you doing here?"

Quickly his eyes took in the figures by the side of the road.

"Not runaway slaves!" he said. "I don't know how you managed to get mixed up in this, but it's something neither you nor I can afford to be caught at. What were you intending to do with them?"

"I was taking them to the Holmes farm," John said.

"Did they ask you to?"

"No, I sent them a note in a basket Aunt Caroline packed for Mrs. Holmes."

"John, you have no idea what you're doing."

To the slaves he said, a note of kindness in his voice, "You can see the light in the kitchen. Good luck, and God bless you." Then, turning back to John, he said, "Jump up behind me, and let's hope everyone is sleeping soundly at Twinoaks."

But as they turned into the curving driveway they could see a light shining through the fanlight over the door. John had no chance to think what he would say, as William propelled him inside.

Aunt Caroline and Uncle Jefferson stood in the lighted hall.

"John," Aunt Caroline said, "where have you been? When I went into your room to make sure your windows were closed, and found you gone, I was out of my mind with worry. What on earth were you doing out in the storm?"

Uncle Jefferson said nothing, but looked at John with even more distaste than at the breakfast table when he had dropped his fork.

"I can explain, ma'am," William said. John was glad somebody could. "I was riding by on my way home and came upon John in the road. He seemed to be in a daze; I think he was sleepwalking."

"Sleepwalking?" Uncle Jefferson said incredulously. "Have you been in the habit of sleepwalking?"

Ann's voice came clearly over the stair railing. "Oh yes, Uncle Jefferson. You'd be surprised what he does sometimes when he's sleepwalking. Mother used to lock his door at night, but we thought he was all over it." Ann hoped the circumstances would justify her falsehood.

"Well, my goodness, why didn't Fanny tell us?" Aunt Caroline fussed. "We're going to get you to bed this minute, and I'll bring you something hot to drink before you catch your death of cold."

John proved Aunt Caroline's point by sneezing all the way upstairs, and the hot drink she brought him felt remarkably good.

After she had finally left his room, satisfied that he would not die of pneumonia that very night, Tom, who had been pretending to be asleep, raised up on one elbow and looked at him, grinning wickedly.

"Well, Yankee John," he said, "what were you really doing? Mother believes everybody, but I don't think sleepwalkers usually get dressed before they sleepwalk. I have a few ideas about what really happened, and it won't be long till I'll be sure."

John closed his eyes and gave a noisy, if unconvincing, snore.

12

XXXXXX

Potions and Poultices

JOHN'S FEVER mounted during the night and before morning Tom called, "Mother, Mother! Come hear what John's saying."

Through the mists of vague comprehension, John felt Aunt Caroline's soft, cool hand on his forehead and tried to think what it was he must tell her. As if from a great distance, he heard Tom say bitterly, "But don't you understand yet? He says he has to get a map to President Lincoln. Why can't you see he just has to be a spy?"

Ann was frantic. How could she keep John from giving away the secret of the map? He also needed a doctor quickly. Without thinking, she insisted urgently, "Shouldn't John have a shot of penicillin right away?"

Tom favored her with a sour glance. "I don't know what that is, but a shot of brandy is what Mother always gives, and she's the best doctor for miles around. She takes care of all the slaves when they're sick, and white folks twenty miles away come to Twinoaks for her herb remedies."

"Don't you have a real doctor?" asked Ann thoughtlessly. Then, afraid she had hurt her aunt's feelings, she added quickly, "Is there anything at all that I can do to help, Aunt Caroline?"

"Yes, dear," Aunt Caroline's voice was low. "Run quickly to the kitchen and tell Aunt Sarah to heat the bricks and flannels. We have a sick boy here." Then, seeing Ann's concerned face in the candlelight, she added, "But I'm right sure he'll be feeling fine soon."

Ann hesitated, disliking the idea of leaving Tom in the room with John, but the decision was taken away from her by Aunt Caroline, whose usually even voice was sharp with urgency.

"I said 'run,' child!" she chided.

The remainder of the day, Ann sat disconsolately in John's room. Nothing anyone could say would persuade her to move, and even Uncle Jefferson came in to remonstrate.

"But you must eat, Ann dear," he declared at lunchtime, and only left her after she promised to come downstairs in the evening if John was better.

Although Tom missed no meals, he equaled Ann in vigilance in watching John through the long afternoon. Each time John muttered the phrase they were all beginning to expect, "The map—must—get—to—Lincoln," Tom leaned closer so he'd be sure not to miss a syllable.

Aunt Caroline looked at her son lovingly and murmured, "He's so worried about his cousin."

Uncle Jefferson looked at his son and struggled against believing the mounting evidence that these were indeed Yankee kinfolk, who, although young, might need watching.

But Ann stared gloomily at Tom and thought, "Hypocrite!"

The next day John was obviously worse. His cheeks were each highlighted with a large crimson spot and his breathing was difficult. He lay back on the white linen pillow and recognized no one, not even Ann.

Mrs. Hurley, hearing of his illness, bustled over

with her favorite remedy. This popular medicine was composed of toads burned to a crisp and powdered. The only good thing about it, Ann decided with sympathetic nausea for John's ordeal, was that it was to be taken in small doses. And Aunt Caroline apparently agreed, for seeing the effect the first spoonful had on John, she turned again to her own herb potions.

Ann could hardly keep back the tears as she rocked slowly in the little chair. John was creating too much interest in the map. Granted that fifty per cent of this raving was discounted and charged only to delirium, it had obviously alerted not only Tom but also Uncle Jefferson and Uncle Lawrence.

She just had to find that map. If Tom did have it, he apparently had no idea what it was. Unaccustomed as she was to browsing through other people's drawers, Ann now took every opportunity when she was alone with John of searching Tom's room. She ruffled rapidly through his stack of handkerchiefs and shirts; she glanced quickly through his underclothes and nightshirts; she poked furtively into every pocket of his suits to no avail and with much dislike, for she remembered he liked to carry small snakes in his pockets.

But the small writing desk in the corner, in which she was most interested, remained always locked.

Finally, one late afternoon, Uncle Jefferson looked into the room as she rummaged desperately through a drawer for the umpteenth time. He raised his eyebrows, but said only, "Perhaps you need more entertainment than you can find here, Ann. If you refuse to leave John, at least allow me to bring you some books to make the hours pass more quickly for you."

Ann managed to answer demurely, "I was looking for John's little prayer book, but I'm afraid I opened Tom's drawer by mistake."

With great relief, she watched Uncle Jefferson's eyes warm perceptibly. "Oh, what a tangled web we weave when first we practice to deceive," she thought. And I'm getting plenty of practice. Somehow Ann's conscience couldn't be quieted by the thought that these lies were necessary.

At this moment, William walked into the room. As if he'd been waiting for just this, John struggled to raise his head and whispered hoarsely, as he had so many times before, "Map—Lincoln!"

Uncle Jefferson and William looked measuringly at each other while Ann tried frantically to create

a diversion. Making the most of her reputation for sheer awkwardness, she managed to overturn the water pitcher and sighed with relief as Uncle Jefferson, trying his gallant best to remember she was a relative, a girl and a guest, hurried from the room before his tongue could betray his irritation.

Ann quieted John by replacing the cool, damp cloth on his hot forehead and then looked questioningly at William. So much depended on his reaction to this crisis. He shook his head at her, but his gray eyes were kind. "Ann," he began, "I don't know what trouble you two are in now, but——"

He was listening to the sound of approaching footsteps. Aunt Phoebe arrived and began to mop up the spilled water. Aunt Caroline rushed in, and putting her arms around Ann, hugged her tightly and crooned, "Poor dear, naturally you're upset, but we're doin' everything possible for your brother. Mrs. Hurley's bringin' over another poultice in the morning and he's jus' sure to be better soon."

Ann allowed some of the ready tears to spill over on Aunt Caroline's comfortable shoulder and was surprised to find that the sympathetic patting did make her feel a bit better.

13

Hide and Seek

As the days passed, Ann grew more and more anxious to have a word alone with John, but no matter what the time of day there was always someone in his room—Aunt Phoebe putting fresh sheets on the bed, Mrs. Hurley holding some sort of bitter-tasting brew to his lips, Aunt Caroline sitting by the window knitting, or Tom watching with an air of sly patience.

John's eyes often met Ann's with a sort of dull hopelessness, but she could not even bring him what news she had gleaned about preparations for war, as Aunt Caroline had decreed that John was not to be worried or excited.

Actually she knew very little. She knew that the slaves were completing the breastworks at Fairfield and that there was a growing feeling of tension. Nearly every evening Uncle Jefferson and Uncle Lawrence went into the library and talked late into the night.

One day as Ann was leaving John's room, her attempt to speak to him defeated this time by Mrs. Hurley, who was stoutly insisting that a little burned salt pork would always create an appetite in an invalid, she met William on the stairway.

"Ann," he said, "will you please talk to me in the library for a moment?"

"Of course," Ann said. Talking to William always gave her a feeling of security.

William sat beside her on the blue sofa by the window and spoke quietly and quickly. "Ann, I'm sure the rest of the family thinks it is delirium and nothing more, but I can't help thinking that there must be some truth behind John's insisting that you and he have a map which must go to President Lincoln. Knowing about the runaway slaves, I can't help suspecting that perhaps somehow you really have managed to find something you think is important, and are foolishly trying to take it north. You'll have to trust me, Ann. Is there such a map?"

Ann hesitated only a moment between her feeling that nobody must know and the feeling that she could not go through another day without confiding in somebody.

"Yes," she said, "we had it, but we don't have it any more."

Just then Belle walked into the library, cool and serene as always in a thin blue dress. "There you are, William," she said. "I've been lookin' all over the house for you."

Knowing Belle wished to speak to William in private, Ann decided to make use of the time and raced up the stairs. She had really become quite adept at managing her petticoats. John was indeed alone but, apparently exhausted by his battle with Mrs. Hurley, had fallen asleep.

"Oh, no," Ann said despairingly. Desperately she shook him, but he only opened one eye and mumbled, "Go away, will you?"

Ann sat down in Aunt Caroline's chair, hoping that John would wake up before anyone came back.

As she sat there she glanced again at the small

writing desk in the corner. Not really expecting it to be unlocked, she tried it idly, and was overjoyed when it opened easily. Quickly she began opening the little drawers at the back of it, one after another. Most of them were empty, and the others contained plenty of small balls of string, nails and pieces of chalk but no literary documents.

She had just opened the last drawer when she heard some small noise from the direction of John's bed. Thinking that John might at last be awake, she turned around to see Aunt Caroline looking at her reprovingly from the doorway.

Again Ann could feel her deciding on what course of action to take as she dealt with this strange Northern niece who concealed hotcakes in her sash and went through other people's desk drawers.

"Ann, dear," she said mildly, "goodness knows what you could rightly expect to find in Tom's desk, but I think it always a good rule not to open anyone's drawers without permission."

Ann reddened, but made no explanation, since she could not think of any plausible reason for looking for anything in Tom's desk.

"We'll say no more about it, dear," Aunt Caroline said. "How nice that John is asleep. Mrs. Hurley means well, but she is wearin'. Last year when I was ill with a fever she insisted on fumigatin' the room with some hot coals on a shovel and set fire to the curtains, and I had to get out of bed and throw a pitcher of water on them."

Ann laughed, wishing with all her heart that she had an Aunt Caroline in her real life. Or was this her real life now?

She was struck with sudden inspiration.

"Aunt Caroline," she said earnestly, "I've been thinking that maybe John would get well faster at home. You're wonderful to us, and we love you for it, but I think when you're sick you always feel better at home where you're used to the way things are."

Aunt Caroline patted Ann's shoulder. "I did talk to your Uncle Jefferson about that, Ann, but he wouldn't hear of it. He says he could not be responsible for sendin' you North now. Any day now—" Tears filled Aunt Caroline's eyes, and she did not finish her sentence.

"I know," Ann said. She really hadn't thought Uncle Jefferson would send them home.

"Why don't you go find Susan and have Percy

saddle up the ponies?" Aunt Caroline asked. "You look almost as pale as John; it wouldn't help for you to be ill too."

Ann went downstairs thoughtfully. She'd been wanting to talk to Susan anyway. She was almost certain now that Tom had not seen the map, and was wondering if Susan might have removed it from the book before Tom took it.

As she reached the library door she was startled to hear William say, "It's no use, Belle. I just can't do it. I don't think the Confederacy is right. I'm not sure the Yankees are wholly right either, but

I've got to get away to think before I do anything. I've almost decided to go to New York to my grandparents' farm. I don't know when I'll be back, and I can't ask you to wait, Belle."

Ann stood outside the library door, incapable of moving.

She heard Belle say slowly, "I do believe in our Confederacy but all my life I've been taught that everyone must act on what he thinks is right. I love you more than ever for havin' the courage to do it, William, but I don't know what to do."

Belle ran out of the library, passing Ann without even seeing her.

Ann decided to go into the library and finish her conversation with William. Just as she entered the room, Susan jumped out of a wing chair which was turned toward a window at the far end of the library and said, "Oh, William, don't go and leave us. Please don't." She was wiping her face with her sleeve.

"Susan," William said, drying her eyes with his handkerchief, "I'll be back one day."

"We might not be here," she said. "John says the South will lose the war, and he and Ann are the only ones who know it for sure."

William exchanged a look with Ann. He held Susan tightly by the arms. "Susan, that's just a silly thing John said, but promise me not to say it to anyone else. You might get John into terrible trouble, and you wouldn't want to do that."

Susan said, "No, I guess I wouldn't."

"I must be getting back to the paper," William said. "I'll see you tomorrow, Ann," he added with special emphasis.

After he had gone, Ann said to Susan, "Susan, do you remember seeing a piece of paper in the algebra book Tom took?"

"Yes, I do," Susan said. "I—oh, fiddlesticks, I left a kitten in the kitchen, and Aunt Sarah said next time she stepped on one she would surely fry it." She ran from the room with the speed of light.

"Susan!" Ann called after her, but Susan was bent on her errand of mercy.

Ann followed Susan all afternoon, but never found her in any place where they could be alone. Even when they went out on the ponies Susan perversely kept half a length ahead of her.

Not until bedtime did Ann feel that the subject of the map could be reopened. "Susan, you said you saw a paper in the algebra book."

"Did I?" Susan yawned, pulled her nightgown over her head and jumped into bed with a flying leap.

"Don't you remember?" Ann asked, trying to make it sound as if it were of little importance.

"Well, I did take it," Susan said defiantly, "and I'm going to keep it, because it's good stiff paper to make paper dolls with."

Ann's heart almost stopped beating. "You—you haven't done it yet, have you? Made paper dolls out of it, I mean?"

"Not yet," Susan said, burrowing under the covers.

"Susan," Ann said, "I like that kind of paper, too. How would you like to trade it for something?"

Susan sat up in bed, bright-eyed. "Well, what?" she asked.

Ann thought quickly. There was no point in offering something from her wardrobe. Susan would not be interested in finery. Then she remembered that her cousin had admired a little white crocheted bag which had been in her portmanteau. She had said it would be just right to carry jacks in.

"How would you like to have my crocheted bag?" she asked.

"Oh, Cousin Ann, I'd purely love it. I'll get you the paper right now."

Susan jumped out of bed and began taking dolls out of the mahogany cradle in one corner of the room. Puzzled, she shook out little quilts and looked under minute pillows.

"That's peculiar," she said. "It isn't here."

"It must be," Ann insisted, helping with the search. But although they took everything out of the cradle, no piece of folded stiff paper was disclosed.

"Oh, pshaw," said Susan. "I did want that little ole bag."

"Think, Susan," Ann said. "Couldn't you have put it somewhere else?"

"No," said Susan positively. "Anything I want to keep I always put in there."

And she jumped into bed again and pulled the covers up to her chin. As far as she was concerned the incident was closed, but Ann heard the grandfather clock chime several times before she went to sleep.

14

ᚷᚷᚷᚷᚷᚷ

Tom Scores His Point

A WEEK later, Aunt Caroline said John was well enough to go downstairs at noon to sit in the sun on the warm porch.

Thin as a shadow but smiling broadly, John swayed as Uncle Jefferson and Uncle Lawrence eased him down the long stairway in a hand swing they had made. He winced as the second step creaked under their combined weights. That night when he had crept out of the house to meet Big Sam seemed years ago. He would probably never know whether or not the two slaves had escaped. Uncle Lawrence had told of two slaves being captured soon after that stormy night. Naturally, it would have seemed suspicious to be too curious, but John hoped it hadn't been the tall Negro with the flashing smile, and his wife Becky. They both deserved their freedom.

The family had been invited to Mrs. Hurley's for the afternoon to watch the slaves work on preparations for the defense of the city. Her porch overlooked a particularly active segment of the breastworks. Aunt Caroline had decreed that although John was much too weak to attempt any social life, he and Ann might have a picnic lunch with Lafe and Aunt Phoebe to watch over them.

The recovery John had made was termed miraculous by the household servants, and even sour old Aunt Sarah had entered into the joyous spirit of the day by volunteering to bake a huge raisin cake.

John's appetite still hadn't returned, and Aunt Caroline was trying all sorts of oddments to tempt his palate. Her favorite tonic was made by pouring boiling water over roots, leaves and blossoms of dandelion plants. This was left to stand until it was very strong, and John had to force a cupful down his throat morning and evening.

John and Ann sighed with relief as the carriage rolled down the drive. Now they could talk.

"We'll simply have to get that map to Lincoln," John said.

Ann nodded. "It just might change the whole course of the war," she agreed. "Maybe we could save thousands of lives by helping the North win the first big battle. But," she added sadly, "you're much too weak to escape even if we had a plan."

"I'll get well fast," her brother promised. "You'll see. Ann, think hard," he begged. "What was the date of that first battle of Bull Run? I know it was after the middle of July, and I seem to remember the twenty-first, but was that it?"

Ann shrugged her shoulders. "Why ask me? I only know that this is the fifteenth of July, and we're surrounded by a loving but suspicious family and thousands of soldiers."

John made an effort to stand, but his knees trembled with the weakness caused by fever and lack of food. "I've got to get well," he groaned, sinking back into the chair. "We're in a desperate state—in more ways than one. I almost wish you hadn't told me all I said about the map." And he held his head weakly in his hands.

Just then Lafe returned with the carriage, and Aunt Phoebe soon appeared with a small basket for

John which she said Mrs. Holmes had sent to tempt his appetite. John smiled ruefully. "Turn about's fair play, they say." His nose turned up at the very thought of more calf's-foot jelly. The name itself was revolting. And he was so tired of arrowroot blancmange.

As Aunt Phoebe left the room, excitement brightened Ann's eyes. "John," she whispered, "let's put a letter under the napkin in the basket when we send it back."

John's eyes were gleaming for the first time since he'd helped Big Sam escape. "Why not?" he chortled. "We've begged Uncle Jefferson so many times to let us go home. It would serve him right if we did manage it by way of the Underground Railway."

Together they composed a note which stated flatly: "We are desperate and we must go home immediately. We have information which can change the course of the war. We beg you to help us!" Signing their names and tucking the letter out of sight, they called Lafe and asked if he could return the basket to the Holmes house that evening before he picked up the family at the Hurley plantation. The dishes could go back later.

John was exhausted, so Lafe carried him upstairs as easily as if he were a baby, and Ann said she'd read to him until he fell asleep.

Later that evening, after John had dozed off into an uneasy nap, Uncle Jefferson stormed into the house in such a temper that Ann shivered and John awoke with a start. They'd never heard him raise his voice before. He'd always prided himself on examining both sides of each question, claiming that that alone would calm a man.

Up the stairway he marched, calling icily for the twins. Ann met him at John's door. Her uncle was obviously furious at them.

"You two!" he shouted, his face almost purple. "What do you mean trying to embarrass me before my neighbors? How could you defy my judgment like that? You could be shot as spies for less!"

Aunt Caroline hurried after him, out of breath. "Really now, Jefferson, remember that John's been very sick. They didn't mean to embarrass you. They jus' didn't think how it would sound to our neighbors. They're jus' thoughtless, homesick children."

Then Tom raced along the hall and spitefully made a face in their direction. "Ha, you're so smart!" he gloated. "I was right all along. Now we'll see what happens to you."

Susan was close on his heels, almost exploding with excitement. "You'll have to eat bread and water for a week, I'll bet," she prophesied darkly.

Belle, worried at the enormity of her father's anger and helpless to prevent the consequences, came in and said pityingly. "He told you it was impossible for you to leave. Why didn't you believe him?"

Ann backed up against John's bedpost for both moral and physical support. "Please," she begged,

although she was beginning to suspect what had happened, "tell us what we did to make you so angry."

Uncle Jefferson snorted in a most ungentlemanly way. "Can you deny writing a note to Ben Holmes begging for help to run away from your own family? It sounded as if you were being held under duress."

Tom couldn't resist a further prick. "Lafe discovered the letter and handed it to me because he thought it was from Mrs. Holmes to you. I knew better and read it."

Oh, you sneak! Ann thought bitterly.

"So I gave it to my father," said Tom smugly.

"And I still believe they've jus' behaved foolishly because they're really homesick," Aunt Caroline again defended them.

"They may be," Uncle Jefferson admitted. "But knowing they're capable of trying to trick me in my own home when I'm merely attempting to keep them from being hurt infuriates me. And as soon as John is able to be out of bed," he continued, turning back to the twins, "you two will be locked in the schoolroom until you can be obedient children again. Maybe writing 'I will be an obedient child' five hundred times will help you remember." He stalked from the room.

"Oh, dear," said Aunt Caroline with a sigh. "I do wish children would think before they act. But then, I suppose that would make them adults, actually."

"And so dull," piped Susan pertly.

"Bedtime for you, miss," announced her mother firmly, and Ann, with a glance of despair in John's direction, followed her aunt and cousin down the hall.

15

XXXXXX

Fire!

"I WILL be an obedient child," Ann's slate read for the forty-fifth time, according to the official tally kept by John, who had only reached thirty-seven.

"Why do you suppose Uncle Jefferson locked the door?" John asked, finishing the word 'child' with a flourish.

"I suppose he thinks he can't trust us any more," said Ann. "Mark up another one for me, John."

"Well, can he?"

"As long as we're locked up in here he can." Ann looked around the dusty schoolroom with loathing. Even in Mr. Tibb's absence his disagreeable personality seemed to fill the room.

"Let's take a break and see if we can't get the window open," she said.

It took all the strength both of them could command to move the heavy, long-closed window. John was breathless. He had not realized how weak he still was after his illness.

"Now that we've got it open what can we do?" John asked crossly. "As soon as we let it go it will just fall down again."

"Wait a minute," said Ann. "Maybe there's a ruler or something in the cupboard."

She opened the cupboard door and sneezed at the odor of chalk combined with dust.

As she was closing the door she caught sight of a small wooden box containing a brightly lithographed paper doll. From under its head protruded one corner of a familiar stiff paper.

"John, look!" she called, sneezing, crying and laughing at the same time.

John was so startled he let the window fall down again, but neither of them cared.

"It really is the map," she said. "Could Susan have carried it up here and forgotten it? She really did want the purse, I think. Or maybe Aunt Phoebe found it. Or——"

"Slow down," John said. "It doesn't matter how it got here, just so it did."

"I suppose not," Ann agreed, tucking the precious paper into her sash. If she ever got home, she decided, she would see if she couldn't have a few sashes. They certainly could be handy.

When they finally managed to open the window again and prop it with the ruler, they stood looking out over the rolling countryside.

"Ann, look," John said sharply, pointing in the direction of Fairfield. Twinoaks was on a high spot, and from their third-floor window they could see fields and roads and houses as from an airplane. And on the roads approaching Fairfield they could see long straggling columns of gray-clad figures.

"What is it?" Ann asked.

"Soldiers," John said, "hundreds of them. They must be getting ready for the Battle of Bull Run." And John shivered as he thought how many of the soldiers would not walk back along the familiar roads.

"John, that means the battle must take place soon, and here we are, further than ever from being able to leave." There were tears in Ann's eyes.

John was still watching the columns of marching

men. Suddenly he said, "Ann, look—they're sending smoke signals."

Ann dried her eyes. "No," she said, "it's too close; the smoke must be coming from Twinoaks—from the stables!"

"Satin Lady and her colt are in there," John said, "and there's nobody outside to notice the fire."

Ann and John both ran to the heavy schoolroom door and beat on it with their fists, calling, "Help! Help! Fire!" But their knuckles soon became bruised and their voices hoarse, and no answer came up the steep stairway.

The smoke was spiraling higher and higher.

"Ann," John said excitedly, "I believe I could get out on the limb of that big tree. It's only about two feet from the window."

"You'd never make it, John," Ann said. "You were out of breath just from opening the window." Then she said reluctantly, "I could, though. I know I could if I didn't have on all these skirts." And resolutely she began to shed first her dress and then her petticoats.

John looked at her with admiration. He knew that Ann, although she was athletic, was afraid of high places.

As long as she could, Ann kept her mind on Satin Lady and her colt and away from the tree with its treacherous branches. As she balanced on the narrow windowsill, John's "about two feet" seemed to grow wider and wider. She couldn't do it. What if she couldn't grab the branch? But she thought she could hear whinnying from the stable, and fresh gusts of smoke gave her new courage.

Fighting the temptation to close her eyes, she jumped. Her fingers closed around the smooth brown branch, but she could feel them slipping. She couldn't hold on; she couldn't. She felt herself falling. There was a crash, and then a tearing sound, and she found herself suspended from a branch fifteen feet above the ground by the seat of her pantalettes.

"Thank goodness they made such strong material a hundred years ago," was Ann's first thought.

Almost immediately she heard a horse trotting up the driveway. "Help, help, fire!" she called at the top of her lungs. She didn't know whether she was more relieved or embarrassed when William rounded the corner of the house. Before he could say a word Ann croaked hoarsely that the stable was on fire. To her chagrin, William disappeared.

Meanwhile John was in a state of frenzy. He ran from the window to the door, to beat hopelessly on it with his hands. Just as he was drawing back his fist for another onslaught the door was opened by Aunt Caroline, bearing the tray of bread and milk ordered for their dinner by Uncle Jefferson. Unable to stop his fist in time, John sent the pitcher of milk flying from the tray.

"Whatever's gotten into you, John?" Aunt Caroline asked in amazement. "Your Uncle Jefferson will be most unhappy at such a display of temper."

Aware of the enormity of his crime, John was unable to speak.

A new thought struck Aunt Caroline. "Where's Ann?" she asked.

All John was able to say was, "In the tree."

"In the tree?" Aunt Caroline's eyes were resting on the heap of petticoats on the floor. "In her pantalettes?" Her voice rose in horror.

However, as John motioned toward the window she could see the smoke above the stable. The stableyard was full of people now, and in a moment William appeared leading Satin Lady. Her head was covered with William's coat, and the little colt followed behind.

Shock followed shock for Aunt Caroline. Close on the heels of discovering her eccentric niece hanging from a tree by her undergarments, she saw her usually proper older daughter run to William, throw her arms around him and kiss his smoke-blackened cheek. Fortunately she could not hear Belle say, "William, I'll even be a Yankee if that's what you want."

Naturally this development so charmed William that it was several minutes before he remembered Ann, who by this time was quite red-faced but growing used to her unusual view of the passing scene.

William arrived with a ladder at the same moment Aunt Caroline appeared from the other direction with a blanket to throw over Ann.

Shortly after that, Uncle Lawrence arrived and had to be told the whole tale. Wiping tears of laughter from his eyes, he said, "This is the first thing in days that has taken my mind off the war."

But Ann suddenly remembered the map, left in her sash in the schoolroom, and hoped that John would have had an opportunity to transfer it to his pocket.

16

XXXXXX

It's William's Move

By mid-july, tempers were becoming even hotter. Soldiers were massing and drilling in every village square. Women still wore the secession colors of gray, blue and red in bonnets, on their dresses, and made into elaborate ornaments which they pinned in their hair.

Soldiers were so numerous around Fairfield that Aunt Caroline decreed there would be no more trips to town for any reason. Worst of all, she forbade even horseback rides or picnics on the plantation grounds.

"We might as well be sick if we're going to be quarantined," Ann grumbled one hot afternoon.

"What's that?" Susan wanted to know.

"Oh, you're a hundred years too young to understand," Ann snapped. Then she felt disgusted with herself for being so edgy with her younger cousin. Everyone was tense these days. Even Uncle Jefferson, after his outburst at the twins, lost some of his reasonable and tolerant attitude, while the tempers of the other members of the household flared more than ever.

Susan insisted on following the twins everywhere. Her kittens had given up playful antics and become dignified full-grown cats, and Susan wanted to be amused.

Ever since the fire and Ann's heroic part in it, Susan had idolized her, and Ann couldn't even wash her hair without Susan insisting on doing the same, regardless of the fact that Aunt Phoebe regularly shampooed her rebellious curls every Saturday morning.

If Ann decided to take a nap, Susan curled up alongside her and dozed. If Ann took a book from the very complete library, and sat down to read, Susan selected Fox's *Book of Martyrs* for the same length of time. At dinner, if Ann refused second helpings, Susan refused them also although it took iron will power. Ann could do no wrong. Hadn't Satin Lady and her colt been saved by Ann?

No wonder Ann's temper grew short. Being raised so quickly to a pedestal was irksome.

John was feeling better physically, although he was still quite thin. He was seldom allowed to listen to the men discussing the mounting numbers of enlistments. They apparently considered him an out-and-out Yankee now, and Tom pointedly ignored him as if he weren't even in the room. This distressed Aunt Caroline, but Uncle Jefferson advised her to let the boys work out their own differences. "There's too much meddling in other people's business nowadays as it is," he asserted.

More and more John turned to William for companionship. They were both outcasts, for William had not yet enlisted, and he continued to be a frequent visitor.

"William," began John one sultry evening, "why don't you just leave and go to New York to your grandparents?"

"I would have gone long ago if it weren't for Belle," William admitted.

"Could you get through the picket lines?" asked John curiously.

"I have given it some thought," William answered slowly. "There are ways, no doubt, that our Quaker friends could show us."

"We're desperate," John confided. "A battle is bound to be fought soon and we have information that could save thousands of lives if we could just get to Washington."

Although William didn't smile at the statement, John felt that he considered it only a boyish boast.

Hoping to arouse William's interest, John plunged on. "Honestly, William, Ann and I found a military map that could mean a lot to the North if they can just get it in time. Why don't the three of us disguise ourselves and try to get through the picket lines?"

William's silence expressed no enthusiasm for any such plan.

"You're miserable here," John went on undiscouraged. "Uncle Jefferson can hardly tolerate me any more. Tom loathes me, and Ann has Susan at her heels every minute of the day."

"I'm afraid your map wouldn't be of much use," stated William doubtfully.

"But if you'd only look at it." John could see refusal in the gray eyes, but he had to go on. This was their last chance for freedom. Besides, he had a private theory that once away from the powerful influences of family and history, he and Ann would regain their accepted place in the twentieth century.

"No!" William's voice was firm. "If I were to leave the South, it would not be as a traitor. I could never betray Virginia, wrong as I believe her to be in seceding. If I were to go north, it would be because of my conviction that the Union is the important thing, not the individual states. The twelve years that I lived in New York with my grandparents have changed my mind about a lot of things, but don't ever show me the map or tell me anything more about it. If I were to take you north, and I'm not promising to do it, it would be to put you on a train for Missouri and nothing more."

John's mind was working quickly. William must be convinced that he was needed in the North, and that he should take the twins with him.

"But your hands are tied here, working on a Southern newspaper. Up North you could fight with a pen for the ideals you believe in, and Uncle Lawrence couldn't tell you what to write."

"That's true," William agreed thoughtfully.

John hardly breathed while William made his decision.

"All right, I'll think it over, at least," he finally announced. "It would take some careful planning, but Ben Holmes has been a good friend of mine ever since I was small. Maybe he would help us."

John was jubilant. "Just wait till I tell Ann! This is what she's been waiting for."

William's smile was more cautious. "We have a long way to go before we celebrate, and it won't be easy," he reminded John.

John's face sobered. "No, I suppose it won't be, but it's worth a good try. Thank you, William. Ann and I will do anything you say," he added, with his fingers crossed.

Their future was now in William's hands.

17

XXXXXX

Swing Low, Sweet Chariot

"SWING LOW, sweet chariot," sang the mourners walking slowly down the dust-covered road behind the horse-drawn wooden hearse. Three light-skinned Negroes sang especially lustily. Although to the casual eye they were simply a part of the sad little group, a closer inspection would reveal that their skins were curiously streaked, and that they were the only ones wearing shoes.

At last the forlorn little cemetery was reached, and the mourners followed the hearse to a freshly dug grave.

One of the procession, a tall straight Negro with white hair stepped forward to conduct the ceremony, which was simple and touching. The one they had come to mourn was an old man who had been much loved, but the speaker comforted them with the thought that Adam had escaped the turmoil of the day to go to his Father's house.

It was almost dark by the time the ceremony was over, and the little knot of mourners left the cemetery while the hearse rattled off in the opposite direction. Who was there to notice that four of the Negroes were now in the back of the cumbersome vehicle, huddled under an ancient and dusty black robe?

As the hearse jolted on through the night, Ann thought wearily that they must be traveling as many miles up and down as they were traveling forward. Trying desperately to keep her mind on something besides her aching bones and the lack of fresh air, she reviewed in her mind the events which had led up to their being in such an improbable place.

When it had been decided that they must leave immediately if they were to escape before war actually began, William had approached Mr. Holmes, fearful that, no matter where his sympathies lay, he would not interfere in his neighbors' affairs.

Fortunately William had spoken at a good time. There was one Negro in whose escape Mr. Holmes was especially interested. His name was George, and when he had stayed behind to help his wife and children to escape months before, Mr. Holmes had promised to help him join them at the first opportunity. Now, he told William, he was too strongly suspected to have anything personally to do with a runaway slave, but at the same time he felt bound by his promise.

Trying to turn over in the cramped space to ease her muscles, Ann remembered how strange they had felt as they waited for a Negro funeral, easing their minds only by the thought of the slave who must escape and the map which they must smuggle out.

The details of parting were still fresh in her mind. That morning a little Negro boy had ridden to the newspaper office and given William a message reading simply, "Tonight." William had immediately dispatched another note to Twinoaks, impressing on the boy that it was to be delivered to no one but Miss Belle.

Ann thought how sad Belle had looked as she called them into her room. In a low voice she had said, "Be ready to leave the instant I get Mother and the others out of the house."

"How are you going to do that?" Ann asked, remembering how Aunt Caroline would hardly let any of them stir beyond the piazza.

"I don't know," Belle said determinedly, "but I'll do it."

"Oh, Belle, will we ever see you again?" Ann asked, remembering all Belle's kindnesses.

"Some day, perhaps, when all this trouble is over," Belle answered soberly.

Ann was convinced that Belle should have been an actress. At dinner that noon she turned to her mother as if she had been struck by a sudden idea. "Let's go callin' this afternoon, Mother," she said. "I declare, I'll lose my mind if I have to sit here knittin' one more afternoon. There certainly won't be any soldiers around between here and the Loomis house, and Susan could go along and play with Cynthia."

"Oh, I don't know, Belle," Aunt Caroline said doubtfully, tempted by the thought of an afternoon's conversation with someone outside the household. "What about the other children?"

"For goodness' sake, Mother, they won't be

alone in the house. And if, as you seem to think, the Yankees' main objective is to capture Twin-oaks, I don't know that we'd be much protection anyhow."

Aunt Caroline smiled. "Well, I guess you're right, Belle. Susan, go tell Aunt Phoebe to help you get dressed, and for goodness' sake tell her to take time to brush your curls properly."

So much for Aunt Caroline and Susan, Ann thought, but what about Tom?

She had underestimated Belle's generalship, however. As the three callers came downstairs in a state of exhilaration at an afternoon away from home, Belle turned to Tom and said, "Tom, dear, would you please ride to town and take this note to William?"

"My goodness, Belle," Aunt Caroline protested. "Let Percy or Lafe do it. John still isn't able to ride, and Tom should stay here and entertain his cousin."

"Tom hasn't been sick," Belle said. "He's a growin' boy and needs some exercise. Besides, he'll be back in half an hour."

Ann thought Belle was emphasizing "half an hour" for their benefit. Half an hour! She thought

Aunt Caroline would never be satisfied with everyone's bonnets and gloves. Five precious minutes were gone before they got into the carriage.

What did one wear when escaping on the Underground Railway? If there was a rule about this Ann had never read it. Something dark—probably the suits they had worn on the train.

While they were dressing, Ann heard the front door slam. Then, to her horror, she heard Uncle Jefferson's voice call loudly, "Caroline! Caroline! Confound it, where is everybody?"

Aunt Phoebe's voice answered soothingly, "They just went callin', sir."

Ann held her breath. If only Uncle Jefferson didn't ask who Aunt Phoebe meant by "they." He'd never leave them alone in the house if he knew about it.

He didn't ask, but disappeared into his study "Oh, please, please make him leave soon," Ann prayed. John slipped into her room, and together they watched the hands move on the small gilt clock on the mantelpiece. Fifteen minutes, then twenty minutes ticked past before they heard Uncle Jefferson call to Aunt Phoebe that he would be home later than usual for supper that evening.

Luckily his departure was faster than Aunt Caroline's.

As she lay in the jolting funeral coach, Ann also thought of the cool, white-washed stable at the Holmes farm where they had made their way as soon as Uncle Jefferson was out of sight.

She remembered how Mrs. Holmes had started to work, blacking their faces with burnt cork, and how shocked she had been when Ann burst into uncontrollable gales of laughter at the sight of John.

"Ann, dear, does thee feel well?" she had asked.

William had arrived shortly before dusk, but their other traveling companion, George—the slave Mr. Holmes had told them about—had not been seen until they arrived at the cemetery.

Ann thought with longing of the cold, cold milk Mrs. Holmes had brought from the springhouse, and of the delicious homemade ginger cookies they had eaten. That led to further thoughts of cold ginger ale and ice cream and steak and French-fried potatoes, but even the thought of food was not comforting to her.

Suddenly the hearse stopped. It was hard to fight the urge to sit up and see what was going on, but they had been warned not to move under any circumstances until their driver told them to.

Then the stifling black blanket was lifted, and they heard the welcome words, "All right."

Stiff-legged and with solemn faces, they climbed to the ground. What they had been expecting they did not know, but what they saw was an enormous haystack.

"Good luck," said the driver, and without another word he drove away into the night.

"What now?" John said, turning expectantly to William. But apparently William was baffled, too.

"I didn't like the driver's looks," Ann said anxiously. "What if he's just abandoned us here in this field?"

"Why a haystack?" John said.

"I imagine, suh," said George, who had not spoken before, "that it's to hide in"—which seemed a sensible suggestion.

The four fugitives began to hollow out a little niche on the side away from the road. Ann's eyes soon filled with tears, and she began to sneeze violently.

"There isn't much use in hiding if you can't control yourself, Ann," William said.

"I cad't help it," Ann said miserably. "I have hay fever. If adybody had told me I would—achoo—have to hide id a haystack I would hab—achoo—hab stayed at Twidoaks."

"Can't you do something, John?" William asked helplessly.

"No," John said, "usually she does that until about the middle of September."

"Longer if I hab to stay here," Ann assured them.

"You might as well go and sit outside," William said bitterly. "If anyone came by now we'd hardly be hidden anyway. Surely someone will pick us up soon."

"I'd as soon be shot as starved to death anyway," John said, picturing the dinner table at Twinoaks with all its abundance.

It seemed half a lifetime before they heard the sound of approaching wheels. They were all ravenous, and Ann, while she was only sneezing occasionally now, was wet and cold from sitting in the damp field.

It was too dark to see the driver, and the only thing he said was, "Step lively." In fact, he was in such a hurry to get started that he shut John's foot in the door.

"Glad it wasn't my head," said John, rubbing his ankle ruefully.

They were almost beyond the point of being hungry now, and had turned their thoughts to soft beds with pillows and blankets. Everyone was too tired to talk, too tired even to worry.

It was still too dark to see well when they finally stopped, but the house they had reached was apparently a rather large one, surrounded by a good deal of ground.

No welcoming light shone out as the door was

opened, and a woman's worried voice said, "Henry, what kept you? I've been out of my mind with worry."

"There was a big party at Gilbert's, and I had to go the long way around so as not to meet anybody."

"Well, hurry in and don't keep them standing on the doorstep," the woman said nervously.

They filed in, feeling like unwanted intruders and wishing there were even a pinpoint of light. But everything was dark.

"Follow me," their driver said.

The woman followed behind the four fugitives, saying, "There are too many soldiers around now; this is the last time. All night I've had a feeling that we should never have tried it again."

"Be careful," the man's voice said. "There are thirteen steps down."

Hand in hand they groped their way downstairs. After the first two or three steps it became a little cooler, and there was a damp, underground smell. They followed through a door their leader had opened. When the door creaked shut again, Ann shivered.

Then a match was suddenly struck and soon a cheerful light glowed from a lamp on a table in the center of the room. On the table was an enormous platter of cold fried chicken, a loaf of crusty white bread, a huge round pat of butter, a pitcher of milk and a fragrant dark-brown molasses cake.

Ann smiled as she noticed that almost the first to move was John, who soon held a drumstick in one hand. Apparently it took only a trip on the Underground Railway to make him forget his grudge against chicken.

Once the bedraggled visitors were revealed as people instead of shadows, their hostess was all solicitude.

"You poor things," she said. "You poor things."

Then her attention was caught by Ann's face. The sneezing and the dampness had given it a distinctly marbled appearance.

"Whatever in the world?" she said, her knife poised in the act of cutting the molasses cake. "Why, you're not slaves."

Suddenly the knife clattered to the floor. She whispered, "You're not—?"

"Spies?" William asked. "No, ma'am." And he told her their reasons for escape. He left out, however, the story of the map.

After they had eaten their fill they began to look around the room, and noticed that around the walls were several straw pallets covered with worn quilts.

"Goodness," the woman said, "there's no real reason why you three can't scrub up now. If anybody saw you they wouldn't know you weren't just relatives."

"Thank you," William said gently, "but if you don't mind I believe we'll just stay as we are. Ann would probably do better to wash and sleep in a real bed, however. She's liable to come down with a cold after our 'outing.' "

So in the end Ann slept in the spare room. She had intended to think about what they would do tomorrow if they reached Washington, but by the time she had pulled the red and white quilt up to her chin she had forgotten everything else except sleep.

Ann was jolted awake by someone shaking her shoulder and saying something about taking potatoes to market.

As they all gathered around the breakfast table, looking rumpled and dirty in their clothes that had once been so immaculate, their hosts explained that if everything was to seem normal the potatoes must be delivered to the market in Washington at the same time as usual.

Once, a statement like this would have brought a dozen questions from Ann and John. Now it seemed a most natural thing that they were to be delivered along with the potatoes.

They were taken to a huge outbuilding housing an enormous wagon with a flat bed. As if unveiling a beautiful painting, Henry stepped to the back of the wagon and proudly opened the flat bed into two parts. Underneath was a space about two feet deep, although so cleverly was it camouflaged that the space was not apparent from the top.

Oh, Ann thought, surely we're not all going to ride in there!

As if he sensed her thoughts, Henry said soothingly, "It isn't far to Washington, but you could never go through the picket lines without a pass."

Soon they were packed into the wagon like clothes in an over-full suitcase, and they could hear the heavy bags of potatoes being thrown in on top of them. It was worse than the funeral coach, because they were not even able to sit up. There were a few small airholes in their prison, but it was stiflingly hot.

After they had been traveling for some time, the wagon stopped, and they could hear voices, apparently arguing. Suddenly Ann felt sure that she was going to sneeze. She struggled to hold it back. Then she realized that the voices were louder, and there was a movement above them as if the potatoes were being shifted or unloaded.

They could hear the voices plainly now. "You're in such an all-fired hurry, could be there's somethin' more than potatoes in your wagon," one of them said.

Henry's voice sounded remarkably unconcerned. "Reckon you won't find anything but potatoes, lessen it might be a few potato bugs."

"We'll keep lookin', case we find us some nice runaway potato bugs," the other voice said.

There was a sound of jabbing and poking. Suddenly some sharp instrument like a pitchfork penetrated the wagon bed for almost six inches. It barely missed George's ear. Nobody moved; there was no room to move even if they dared. Besides, who knew where the weapon would strike next?

In another moment or two there came, miracu-

lously, the welcome sound of potatoes being thrown back into the wagon. They began to move forward.

Before long the wagon stopped again, but this time there were no strange voices, only Henry saying matter-of-factly, "Reckon you might as well come out. We're in Washington."

Ann could not repress a giggle. Wouldn't Aunt Hattie Lou be surprised if she could see them returning triumphantly to Washington on top of a load of potatoes—dirty and disheveled and planning to speak to the President of the United States!

18

XXXXXX

Two Southern Yankees

THE TWINS would have known President Lincoln anywhere, they had seen his pictures so often in their history books. "Although," observed John afterward, "his eyes weren't so sad as most of his portraits show."

Ann and John, by sheer perseverance, had managed to get close enough to the President to capture his attention. At the sight of the disheveled twins Lincoln, always interested in people, had stopped on his way to his carriage—to the consternation of his bodyguard.

"Are you twins?" he asked, stepping over in front of them.

"Yes, indeed, President Lincoln," they replied in perfect chorus—to his evident amusement.

"Do you always speak together and say the same thing?" he continued, his interest aroused.

"Oh, no, sir!" they chorused again, and the President's eyes twinkled.

"Please, Mr. President," interrupted a stern-faced colonel. "You'll be late for the rally if you don't hurry."

A look of sadness crossed Lincoln's face, and the twins noticed how weary he suddenly looked.

"These young people apparently have something to tell me," he stated firmly, not moving. "Now, what is it? As the gentleman says, we are on our way to a meeting and time is at a premium." He turned to John, who was quite grimy from his ride in the potato cart, and asked humorously, "Do you want my permission to enlist?"

"No, sir. I mean I'm hardly old enough yet," John stammered. "But we have a map for you, sir."

The President smiled at them pleasantly. "Now, just how can this map of yours help me?"

"It's a detailed map of the land around Fairfield, Virginia, sir." John's voice was shrill with excitement. "And we hope it can help the North win the

first battle of the war and end it all sooner and save lives for both sides."

The colonel's eyes narrowed. "How did you know there was to be a battle in that vicinity, young man?"

John thought fast. "We just came from there, sir, and from all the troops around there and all the entrenchments being dug, it looks as if something is going to happen, and we want to help in some way."

Lincoln's eyes were staring into the future as he replied kindly, "Indeed, anything that will help to save lives is of the utmost importance." Turning to the impatient colonel, he ordered, "Take this map and check it against the ones we have. Perhaps there will be something of value to us. We certainly can use valid information about that section of the country."

Then, smiling down on Ann and John from his great height, he added reflectively, "Seeing the patriotism of you young people does make it all seem worth while. Thank you for coming to see me with your map."

This time, the colonel was successful in steering the President into his carriage. But to John's and

Ann's dismay, the precious map for which they had risked their lives was last seen being stuffed into a side pocket of the officer's uniform.

"I wonder if he will ever look at it again?" said Ann.

"I'm still sure it can help," John insisted. "Anyway, we've done our best." And within minutes, the whole episode was over.

"President Lincoln looks as if he's carrying the whole weight of the war on his shoulders," Ann remarked as they watched the carriage drive away.

"Yes, he looks tired already," agreed John, "and just think, the war has three more awful years to go unless our map stops it. Well, not everyone who comes to Washington to see the Lincoln Memorial sees President Lincoln instead."

"Wouldn't Aunt Hattie Lou disown us?" laughed Ann.

"I wonder if there's an 1861 version of her?" John said. "But let's not stop to find out!"

Ann became practical. "What do we do now?"

"Find a train heading for Missouri, of course," John replied immediately.

Ann was hesitant. "Will it be Missouri 1861 or Missouri 1960?"

"Whichever it is, we'll be farther away from the war!" And John led the way confidently to the station.

Trains didn't run on schedule in 1861, the twins discovered, but fortunately there was a train waiting to go west—even as far as Missouri, the conductor admitted—if the rails were still intact. Henry had pressed some money into John's hand before he rattled off with his potato wagon, so buying tickets was no problem.

Boarding the train was one of the happiest moments the twins had ever experienced. Although the train was still one of Lincoln's era, John insisted that if they closed their eyes for a long time, they'd wake up in the twentieth century.

"Close your eyes tightly and concentrate on home and Mother and 1960," John ordered. "And don't open them 'til I pinch you."

"That makes sense," Ann remarked. "That's where we both came in."

They tried to relax, and as the minutes passed and the bumping of the car became less noticeable, they fell into a deep sleep.

The porter woke them finally. "End of the line. St. Louis. Everybody out." And John and Ann blinked at the unaccustomed brightness of electric lights.

"Shades of Thomas A. Edison!" gasped John. "I believe we made it!"

Ann's ankles felt cold and she almost blushed as she looked down and saw not a single ruffle. Hopefully, she turned to look at John and sighed with relief seeing his normal suit and shirt, but modern clothes certainly did seem skimpy now.

"Did you just now dream you lived during the War Between the States, too, or were we really living in that time?" Ann asked shakily.

John's answer came slowly. "We'll really never know."

At Ann's gasp, John followed her gaze to the open toe of her shoe. There, just barely showing, was the black velvet ribbon that they had first seen tied around the fateful map, the ribbon Ann had stuffed into the toe of her traveling boot.

John's whoop of delight startled Ann. "That proves we actually were displaced in time and I'll bet we can do it again any time we want to!"

"For goodness' sake, John," his sister scolded. "We're not even home yet from this adventure. Let's enjoy our own age and its conveniences until we rest up a bit. I, for one, am anxious to push some buttons to make toasters pop and lights turn on and fans buzz. And most of all, to take a bath all over at the same time."

"All right," said John agreeably, but there was a glint of pure joy in his eye.

"We're really home," said Ann, looking happily out the window at the familiar station. Home! It had a wonderful sound. They were Southern Yankees no longer.